STRANDED

A NOVEL BY

SILK WHITE

Good2go Publishing

This novel is a work of fiction. All the characters, organizations, establishments, and events portrayed in this novel are either product of the author's imagination or are fiction.

GOOD2GO PUBLISHING
7311 W. Glass Lane
Laveen, AZ 85339
Copyright © 2013 by Silk White
www.good2gopublishing.com
twitter @good2gobooks
G2G@good2gopublishing.com
Facebook.com/good2gopublishing
ThirdLane Marketing: Brian James
Brian@good2gopublishing.com
Cover design: Davida Baldwin
Editor: Kesha Buckhana
Typesetter: Harriet Wilson
ISBN: 9780989185950
Printed in the United States of America
10 9 6 7 6 5 4 3 2 1

BOOKS BY THIS AUTHOR

Married To da Streets
Tears of a Hustler
Tears of a Hustler 2
Tears of a Hustler 3
Tears of a Hustler 4 – You've Been Warned
Tears of a Hustler 5 – The Spades
Teflon Queen
Teflon Queen 2
Never Be the Same
Stranded

ACKNOWLEDGEMENTS

To you reading this right now. Thank you for stepping inside the bookstore, stopping by the library, or downloading a copy of Stranded. I hope you have enjoyed this read from top to bottom. My goal is to get better and better with each story. I want to thank everyone for all their love and support. It is definitely appreciated! Now without further ado ladies and gentleman, I give you **"Stranded"**. ENJOY!

PROLOGUE

Michael's eyes shot open like he had just been brought back from the dead. He blinked twice as his vision slowly came back. "Hey," he said in a frail, dry, and scratchy voice. "What's going on?" Michael asked nervously as he looked up and noticed that he was surrounded by a room full of big strong looking white men. Each white man had a no nonsense look on their face and a sharp killing instrument in their hand.

Michael tried to sit up and move his arms and legs, but quickly realized that they were strapped down to the table he was laying on top of. Michael looked around nervously from face to face until he recognized one of the white faces. "Tom!" He squinted his eyes to get a better look. "Tom! What's going on? Untie me," Michael said with his eyes pleading and begging Tom to untie him and let him free. Michael lifted up his neck and saw his wife and daughter lying dead on the floor in a pool of their own blood. Immediately Michael knew he was in trouble and more than likely going to die. "Tom, what's this all about? I thought we were cool?"

"Cool?" Tom echoed looking down at Michael like he was insane. "You people just don't get it do you?" Tom chuckled. "You people think just cause you got a black president that y'all can run around like y'all running shit." Tom paused for a second. "Well Michael I'm here to personally tell you that the only thing you people run is your mouths," he said removing a brand new shiny ax from behind his back.

Michael's eyes widened with fear when his eyes came in contact with the ax that Tom held in his hand.

"Listen Tom," Michael began. The only way Michael would be able to get away from the crazy white men was to talk his way out. "You don't want to do this."

"Yes, I do."

"Trust me, if you kill me you'll have hundreds of people out here looking for me by the morning," Michael bluffed. "Let me go and you'll never hear from me again; I promise."

"No one even knows that you're here." Tom smiled as he gripped the ax with two hands.   "Why are you doing this? Is it cause I'm black?" Michael asked.

"Yes," Tom answered quickly. "I can't stand you ignorant motherfuckers and I'm tired of y'all just being here on earth just taking up space." The look on Tom's face said that he was disgusted and the more Michael spoke the angrier he was becoming.

"Ignorant?" Michael repeated. "I have a Master Degree, I'm the manager at my job that pays six figures, and I'm the owner of several small businesses," he said to let Tom know that he was about his business and that he shouldn't judge a book by its cover.

"The only thing you are my friend..." Tom paused and smiled wickedly down at Michael, "is **STRANDED!**" he said as he swiftly lifted the ax up over his head and brought it down chopping Michael's head clean off his shoulders. Tom didn't stop there. He continued to swing the ax like a mad man until there was blood everywhere and Michael's body was chopped up into little bloody pieces. Once Tom was done, his buddies quickly grabbed Michael's chopped up body parts and tossed them into a potato sack bag. Tom grabbed the potato sack and carried it outside and dropped it down in the middle of the driveway. One of his buddies quickly handed him a plastic canister of gasoline. Tom poured gasoline all over the potato sack, lit a match, and tossed it down on what was once Michael's body. Tom and his buddies looked on as the potato sack erupted in bright orange flames. Tom's wife Ann came out the house and smiled when she saw the potato sack in flames.

"Another one bites the dust," Ann chuckled as if seeing the potato sack on fire was amusing to her. "I love it."

"You haven't seen nothing yet!" Tom's voice boomed. "The next pack of niggers I catch, I swear to God..." He shook his head. "I swear to God, I'm going to do them so bad that they

STRANDED

WELCOME HOME

Dez splashed a handful of water on his face as he looked up at his reflection in the dingy mirror in his cell. After a long ten year bid, today was the day that he was finally going to be released and let back out into society. Dez would have been lying if he said that he wasn't nervous about being released. The only thing that helped him out was knowing that he had a beautiful wife and two beautiful children waiting for him on the outside. Two red faced C.O.'s came banging on Dez's cell door with their night sticks.

"Hey Barkley, you ready to go?"

Dez nodded, grabbed all of his pictures, legal papers, and his bible. He had already given away all of his other personal belongings out to a few other inmates on the compound. The two C.O.'s escorted Dez to a small office where he had to fill out his release form. He was then given a jail ID and a forty dollar check.

"Try not to spend all that in one place," one of the C.O.'s joked as he opened the front door. "I'll see you again in a month," the other C.O. said as him and his partner burst out into laughter. Dez ignored the two idiots and smoothly bopped out of the prison gates never looking back. Dez didn't have a clue what he was going to do with his life, but the one thing he did know was that under no circumstances was crime an option. He had just gave the system ten long years of his life. Ten years that he would never be able to get back, ten years of pain and suffering. Dez didn't care if he had to get a job at McDonald's as long as it wasn't illegal, he was all in. He was even willing to scrub toilets and mop floors if he had to. Living a civilian's life and making an honest living was his goal. Dez's entire face lit up when he saw his wife Pamela leaning up against the hood of the black 2002 Explorer with a huge smile on her face.

"Heeeeeey Baby!" Pam yelled excitedly as she ran and jumped into Dez's strong arms. Ten years of being in jail and lifting weights had Dez's body looking like something special. "Oh my god. I've missed you so much!" Pam said admiring Dez's huge muscles.

"I missed you too baby," Dez said with his eyes closed. He inhaled Pam's scent and at the moment it didn't even feel real. He had dreamed of this day so many nights while in his cell and now that the time had come it didn't even feel real. Dez felt like any second someone would wake him up, because he had to be dreaming right now.

"Look at you with your big muscles and what not," Pam beamed. Her face was filled with love and excitement.

"These old things?" Dez smiled as he flexed, making his chest jump. First the right one then the left. Pam gave Dez a super wet sloppy kiss.

"Let's get up outta here before these motherfuckers try to put me back in jail," Dez said and then hopped in the passenger seat of the Explorer.

Pam and Dez talked and laughed for the entire ride back to the city. Pam also showed Dez recent photos of his two children. His son little Dezzy was now twelve years old and a spitting image of him. While Dez was incarcerated he spoke to little Dezzy often on the phone and Pam would always bring little Dezzy up to the jail to visit his father. On the other hand Dez's daughter Trina was a whole other story. She was sixteen going on twenty-nine and couldn't stand her father. In her eyes she didn't have a father, didn't need one, and definitely didn't want one.

Dez stared down at Trina's picture and smiled. No matter what, she was still his daughter. When he used to call home Trina always refused to get on the phone and speak to him. At first Dez was angry and upset that his daughter didn't wish to speak to him, but he realized that he had been absent from her life for the past ten years and knew he had a rough road ahead of him.

"I know Trina's still mad at me for not being around when she needed me the most," Dez said out loud still staring down at the photo in his hand. "But I promise to make things right this time around." Dez was determined to earn his daughter's love back by any means necessary.

"Trina's been really showing her ass lately," Pam told Dez. "She thinks she's grown since she turned sixteen. Every boy she wants to date is all heading down the wrong path. They are either drug dealers or gang members."

"I'll take care of it," Dez said. The more Pam told Dez about Trina, the angrier Dez became. He couldn't believe his daughter was out in the streets showing her ass and running around with the wrong crowd like she didn't have no sense. Dez knew getting back into Trina's life was something he couldn't just jump right into. It was going to be a process. No matter how long it took Dez planned on sticking around until his mission was accomplished. He'd be damned if he just spent ten years in jail, just to come home and let his family fall apart.

"I was thinking," Pam said looking over at Dez. "I think we should do something as a family."

"Something like what?"

"I was thinking maybe Disney World," Pam smiled. "It will be fun."

"I just got out of jail and my funds ain't looking too good right now," Dez said honestly. "And I wouldn't want to put all that on you. Plane tickets and all that… Nah let me get a job first, get back on my feet, and then maybe we can go on a vacation."

"Stop worrying about money baby. I can pay for it," Pam smiled. She was just happy to have her husband back home and her face couldn't hide it. "I was thinking maybe we could make this a road trip."

"A road trip?" Dez repeated. He wasn't too fond of the idea of a road trip.

"Yes, a road trip," Pam said pulling into the driveway of their small house. "I think that would be a good way to get you and Trina back speaking again," she said opening the front door to the house and stepping inside. "With you two being stuck in the car together for all those hours, you two will have no choice, but to speak to each other." Dez smiled. He had to admit the road trip idea didn't sound too bad especially once Pam broke it down to him. Whatever Dez had to do to get his family back in order was a done deal.

"I'm all in," Dez said pulling Pam in close for a kiss. Dez's hands began to explore Pam's nice voluptuous body. Their lip lock was quickly interrupted when Pam saw little Dezzy hop off the school bus from the kitchen window.

"Your son is here," Pam said pushing Dez up off of her. She quickly fixed her clothes before the young man burst in catching them in the act.

Little Dezzy walked through the front door and immediately his eyes lit up in shock when he saw his father standing in the kitchen next to his mother. "Daddy!" he squealed as he ran and jumped in his father's arm.

Dez hugged his son tightly and spun him around a few times before sitting him down. "Damn look how big you are," Dez said smiling from ear to ear. "What they feeding you in school?"

For the rest of the day Dez and little Dezzy sat in front of the T.V. playing video games. Little Dezzy schooled his father and explained and taught him how to play all of the latest video games until dinner was ready. Pam had cooked steak, mashed cheese potatoes, and string beans. Pam said a quick prayer before the trio dug down into their food. Dez was happy and thankful to taste a home cooked meal. It had been so long since he'd had "real food" that he didn't even realize that he had all eyes on him due to all the loud smacking he was doing.

"I know my cooking is good, but damn!" Pam said as her and little Dezzy fell out laughing. "Slow down baby, there's plenty more where that came from,"

Dez smiled and looked up at the clock that rested on the wall that read 9:45 p.m. Instantly Dez's mind wondered where Trina was and what time would she be coming home? Now that he was home a lot of things would be changing around here for the better. "Trina doesn't have a curfew?" Dez asked with a raised brow, nodding at the clock that rested on the wall.

"She usually is home by now. Let me call her cell phone and find out where that girl is." Pam stood up and stopped dead in her tracks when she heard loud music. Immediately she knew that was Trina. Pam peeked out the kitchen window and saw an old school car with big shiny rims pulling in the driveway behind her Ford Explorer. 2Chainz song "Crack" bumped loudly from the speakers causing the trunk on the old school car to rattle violently. Seconds later the music stopped the sound of two people laughing could be heard followed by keys jingling. Trina and a guy that looked like an obvious drug dealer walked through the front door smelling like weed.

"That shit was crazy right?" Trina spoke loudly as her and her male friend headed down the hall towards her bedroom not bothering to speak to anyone.

"Um, excuse me!" Dez's voice boomed causing Trina and her male friend to stop dead in the middle of their tracks. He slowly pushed away from the table and walked over towards Trina and her friend. "Wassup?" Dez asked looking at Trina. "Y'all just walk up in here and don't speak to nobody?"

"Yo Dez, I don't really got time for all this." Trina yawned and then headed towards her bedroom until a firm hand on her shoulder stopped her progress. Trina quickly spun around and smacked Dez's hand off of her shoulder. "Don't put ya fucking hands on me!"

Before Dez even realized it, his arm shot out in a flash and his hand wrapped around Trina's throat as he forced her back up against the wall. Trina's body made a rough sounding noise when it came in contact with the wall. "Who the fuck you talking to like that?"

"Dez please don't hit her," Pam called out from the kitchen.

"Yo my man what you doing!?" Trina's male friend said as if he had an attitude. Dez quickly turned and faced Trina's male friend that favored the rapper Lil' Boosie like he was crazy. Before anybody could stop him, Dez snuffed Trina's male friend and beat him all throughout the house like he had disrespected or violated his mother. After Dez was done whipping the young punk's ass he violently tossed him out the front door like Jazzy Jeff from the Fresh Prince. Once that was all said and done, Dez returned his focus back on Trina.

"So this what you do while I'm gone? Huh?" Dez barked. "You disrespect your brother and mother, come home any time you feel like it, and bring drug dealers up in our home. That's what you do?"

"Listen Dez," Trina began. "You can't just come home after being gone for ten years and think you can tell me what to do. That's not happening!"

"First off my name is Daddy, not Dez."

"I don't got no Daddy. Never have and I never will Dez," Trina spat. "My Daddy died a long time ago." Dez smacked the shit out of Trina before she could even finish her sentence.

"Who the fuck you think you talking to like that!?!" Dez barked.

"I hate you!" Trina yelled as she spit on Dez and ran to her room and slammed the door behind her. Dez looked down and saw that the spit had landed on his shirt. He was getting ready to kill Trina until Pam stopped him.

"Baby please," Pam pleaded. "Leave her alone before you wind up really hurting that girl."

Dez exhaled loudly, and then headed to him and Pam's bedroom to cool off before he did something he'd wind up regretting later. Dez flopped down on the bed and buried his face in his hands. A lot of things had changed since his absence. Before Dez got locked up Trina was a little princess that couldn't do any wrong. Every other word out of her mouth was Daddy this and Daddy that. Now ten years later the first thing out of her mouth was she didn't have a Daddy and that's what killed Dez the most. He knew if he hadn't be sitting in jail for the past ten years and instead had been home with his family things would be way different right now. If Dez could go back in time and change things, he definitely would.

"You alright?" Pam asked placing a hand on Dez's shoulder.

"I've been better," Dez said dryly staring down at the floor.

"Once Trina gets used to you being back around, things will get back to normal," Pam said speaking in faith.

"How did you let Trina get so out of control like this?" Dez asked looking up at Pam. Of course it wasn't all Pam's fault, but unlike Dez she was around and active in Trina's life for the past ten years.

"Raising two kids by yourself ain't easy," Pam said matter of factly. "If you were here, yes a whole lot of things would be different, but you weren't here and I did what I could with what little I had."

"I know you did baby," Dez said while pulling Pam in for a hug. "You did a wonderful job and I'll never leave your side again. You got my word on that."

"You promise?"

"I promise," Dez said as he kissed Pam and slowly began unbuckling her pants.

"No baby. We can't. The kids are still awake," Pam said as her breathing went from desperate to choppy. Dez slowly pulled Pam's pants and thong down to her ankles and made her bend over and grab the bed for support. Before Pam got a chance to protest, she felt Dez lapping over her clit from behind. Dez spread Pam's ass cheeks apart as he tasted her wet peach from behind loving and savoring Pam's taste. He had waited ten years to taste that sweet pussy again and now Dez planned on taking full opportunity of the situation.

Pam reached behind her pushing Dez's face even further into her wet slice. She shifted her hips while rubbing her ass crack up and down Dez's nose and face, and then released a slow long moan. The loud slurping that came from between her legs only turned Pam on even more. Greedy sounds came from her over and over as she moaned. Dez quickly pushed Pam down on the bed, turned her over, put her on her knees, with her face in the pillow, pulled her ass back towards him, and wrapped his hands firmly around her waist as he roughly entered her from behind. There was a raging furnace between Pam's legs. She jerked and tightened her thighs as Dez plunged in and out of her wetness. Dez watched her and felt her enjoy her orgasm just as much as she did.

"I want to suck it," Pam said in a husky voice. She turned around looking up at Dez as she slowly wrapped her full lips around his pipe. Pam slurped Dez's dick nice and slow. Pam's

11

moans told Dez that she wanted more. Dez quickly fucked Pam's mouth like it was a pussy. He firmly held the sides of Pam's head with both hands as he fed her dick. He slid in and out of her mouth until he couldn't take it no more and spilled his energy.

"Oh my God!" Dez huffed breathing heavily. That's just what he needed to take his mind off of his problems for the moment. Dez laid down for a few minutes then quickly sat up and looked at Pam.

"What?" she asked defensively.

"I think the road trip idea," Dez paused. "I think that will be a good idea after all."

Pam smiled, threw on a pair of sweat pants and a wife beater, and then slid down onto Dez's lap. "I think it's a great idea and I also think you and Trina need this trip. Just please have patience with her."

Dez nodded.

"So it's official then; tomorrow the Barkley family will be going on our first road trip." Pam smiled with an excited look on her face. She was just happy to have her husband back home. With Dez back home her family was now complete.

Dez nudged Pam up off of his lap as he stood up. "I'm gonna go apologize to Trina," he said then exited the bedroom. Dez reached Trina's bedroom, took a deep breath, and then knocked on the door.

"Go away!" The voice on the other side of the door yelled. Dez ignored Trina and entered her room anyway. Trina looked up at Dez and sucked her teeth. "What you want now? Damn!"

"I just wanted to apologize," Dez said humbly. "I know I've been gone for ten years, but I'm still your father and you will respect me."

"You finish?" Trina asked rudely.

"What's your fucking problem!?"

"Yo, you blowing my shit right now!" Trina faked a yawn. It took everything inside of Dez not to smack the shit out of his daughter again, but her nasty ass attitude was really starting to work his nerves.

12

"We're going on a road trip in the morning," Dez told her. "Pack a couple of things. We probably gonna be gone for the whole weekend."

"Hmmp!" Trina hummed. "I ain't going," she said as if she was the adult and Dez was the child.

"It's a family road trip and last time I checked you were still a part of this family, so you're going."

"I don't want to be a part of this family so I ain't going," Trina countered.

"You going and that's that!" Dez barked. "This ain't up for discussion. Be ready in the morning and have your shit packed," he said and then exited Trina's room leaving her sitting there looking stupid. The one thing Dez had to work on was his temper. Between Trina's smart ass mouth and her nasty attitude he knew the most difficult part about the road trip was going to be not killing his daughter. Dez left his daughter's room and went to check on little Dezzy. Dez peeked his head inside his son's bedroom and saw Dezzy lying under the covers in his bed sleeping peacefully. Dez smiled and watched his son sleep for a couple of minutes. Whether he liked it or not this was his family and it was his job to take care of them by any means necessary and take care of them is just what Dez vowed to do even if it meant losing his own life.

ROAD TRIP

The next morning Dez loaded the Ford Explorer with their luggage. He was excited about the road trip to Disney World, but he was even more excited just to be spending quality time with his family. After being incarcerated for so long and then released, Dez felt like this was his second chance at life and an opportunity to make up for lost time.

Pam stepped out the house wearing a tight pair of black jeans, a white wife beater, and a pair of flip flops. Her hair was pulled back into a ponytail and an oversized pair of designer sunglasses rested on her face.

"Good morning baby." Pam kissed Dez on the lips and then hopped in the driver seat behind the wheel. "I'll drive until I get tired and then you can take over from there."

"No problem," Dez replied as he saw little Dezzy out the house with a big smile on his face.

"Hey Daddy," Dezzy squealed giving his father a fist bump.

"You ready to have some fun?"

"Yup," Dezzy answered quickly then climbed in the back seat.

Twenty minutes later Dez walked to the front door and yelled into the house. "Trina bring ya ass on!"

Three minutes later Trina stepped out the house wearing a pair of black Good2Go leggings with red letters going across her ass, a black spandex fitting halter top, and on her feet were a pair of four inch black pumps and just like her mother an oversized pair of designer sunglasses covered her eyes.

"You ain't going nowhere with me looking like that," Dez huffed. "You might as well turn right back around and go change them clothes. We going on a family vacation; not to the club."

Trina sighed loudly, rolled her eyes, ignored her father, and hopped in the back seat slamming the door purposely for extra emphasis just to fuck with Dez and upset him even more.

"Baby don't," Pam pleaded. "Let her wear what she wants. Let's just enjoy our trip."

Dez wanted to spazz out and rip his daughter's head off, but Pam was right. The plan was for them to have a good time and enjoy the trip; not to be fussing and arguing the entire time. Dez planned on keeping his mouth shut for now, but later when he got Trina alone he planned on giving her an ear full. Once everyone was situated, Pam pulled out of the driveway and followed the directions the GPS on her iPad gave her.

Trina sat in the back seat with her face crumbled up. Her attitude was evident. She wasn't happy and the last place on earth she wanted to be was trapped in a car with her family. Pam and Dezzy were cool. It was Dez that she couldn't stand. Trina was still upset that Dez had put hands on her new boyfriend last night. After being gone for ten years, who did he think he was to just come in and tell her what she could and couldn't do... As far as Trina was concerned, Dez was a stranger to her and she couldn't stand him. Instead of being a father Dez wanted to break in rich people's houses and rob them blind. Just the thought of the whole thing disgusted Trina.

"You aight back there?" Dez asked looking behind him. Dezzy smiled and nodded his head yes while Trina sucked her teeth, stuck her earphones in her ears, and turned up the volume on her iPod. Whatever Dez had to say Trina didn't want to hear it.

Pam glanced over at Dez, gave him a wink, and mouthed the words I love you. Before they left the house Pam gave Dez all of the money that they would be spending on the trip. She knew Dez was used to being a provider and didn't want him feeling like less of a man because his funds were low. It was the little things like that, which made Dez love Pam the way that he did. Pam and Dez had been together for seventeen years and their love was still as strong as ever and getting stronger and stronger every day.

"My eyes are starting to get a little tired," Pam said pulling over to the side of the road. "You mind taking over for a few hours?"

"I got you," Dez said as him and Pam switched positions. She took up the passenger seat and Dez slid behind the wheel and got back on the highway blending in with the rest of the cars on the road. Within the next thirty minutes the entire car was asleep. As Dez cruised along the highway he noticed it start to pour down raining. He quickly turned on the windshield wipers and then glanced at the directions on the iPad. Being in jail for such a long time Dez didn't really understand how to work the iPad and he didn't want to wake Pam up from her sleep. Dez quickly reached over to the glove compartment and removed a road map. He was from the old school and wasn't hip to all this new technology, iPads, GPS Systems and all that. The road map would have to do. Dez kept the wheel straight and unfolded the map on his lap. The hard rain coming down didn't make things any easier for Dez. He struggled to see through the wet windshield as his eyes took turns glancing through the windshield, then back down to the map that rested on his lap.

"Shit!" Dez cursed when he realized he missed his turn. The rain and the road map were starting to confuse him. It had been years since he read or even looked at a map and honestly he didn't even want or feel like driving any more, but he knew his wife was tired and needed to rest so he had no choice but to thug it out. As Dez continued to drive he heard a loud knocking noise coming from under the hood followed by a cloud of smoke. The loud knocking noise caused everyone in the car to wake up. The smoke rising from the engine made it impossible for Dez to see anything, having no other choice he quickly pulled over to the side of the road.

"What happened?" Pam asked with a nervous look on her face. She looked at the GPS on the iPad and saw the GPS had gave them an alternate route which meant that Dez had got lost or missed a turn at some point. "Where are we?"

"I have no idea," Dez answered honestly.

"Oh my God!" Trina huffed from the back seat with an obvious attitude. "Bad enough I gotta be stuck with him, but now I gotta be stuck with him on the side of the road! What else could go wrong?"

Dez ignored Trina and did his best to keep his mouth shut as he stepped out into the rain. He had to remove himself from out the car before he reached back and slapped the shit out of Trina. Dez opened the hood and looked inside. He didn't know shit about cars, but figured why not take a look anyway. Once the smoke cleared Dez didn't have a clue what he was looking at. All he saw was the engine and a bunch of wires. Not knowing what else to do, Dez figured maybe the engine or something might have just needed to cool off. Just as Dez got ready to hop back in the Explorer he spotted a tow-truck slowing down behind the Explorer.

A big white man stepped out the tow truck and headed towards Dez. His big black combat boots splashed loudly on the wet ground as he slowly made his way over. "Seems like you could use a little help," the white man said with a smile. "Mind if I take a look?"

"Be my guest," Dez said nodding towards the engine. He glanced at the name tag on the white man's blue mechanic suit and read the name Tom. After examining the inside of the hood for about two minutes the white man removed his head from under the hood and said, "It's your transmission." The white man extended his hand. "The name's Tom by the way."

"Dez," Dez replied as the two shook hands.

"I have my own mechanic shop a few miles down the road," Tom announced. "I could tow your truck to my shop and get this thing fixed first thing in the morning if you like. We have a bad storm headed this way, so I won't be able to do anything with your truck until morning."

"That's very nice of you Tom, but that sounds like it might be kind of expensive and honestly I don't have the money right now to get my truck towed or fixed," Dez explained.

"Tell you what I'm going to do," Tom said looking Dez in his eyes. "No way am I going to leave you and your family out here on the side of the road, so why don't I give y'all a tow to my house. Y'all can dry off and get something to eat, then first thing in the morning me and you can take the Explorer to my shop and I'll have one of my workers fix it free of charge. What do you say?"

Dez looked at Tom for a second thinking it over before he replied. "I don't know about that," he said sounding a little skeptical. He had just been released from an upstate correctional facility and knew just how racist *some white people could be.* "I don't like the feeling of owing somebody something. Know what I mean?"

"Dez you don't owe me nothing," Tom said convincingly. "I'm doing this out of the kindness of my heart. I see a man and his family stranded on the side of the road and all I'm trying to do is help. You can take it or leave it. It's up to you."

Dez stood there for a second as loud thunder boomed from the sky and the raindrops came down even harder.

"I told you it was a bad storm passing through tonight," Tom reminded him as the two men stood in front of the Explorer getting drenched.

"Give me a second to talk it over with my wife," Dez said walking around the Explorer and hopping back in the driver's seat.

"Can he fix it?" Pam asked right away.

"Yes he can, but he won't be able to fix the truck until the morning," Dez explained. "He said it's supposed to be a bad storm passing through tonight."

"So what are we supposed to do until the morning?" Pam asked nervously with panic evident in her voice. The last thing she wanted to do was spend a night on the side of the road in the middle of nowhere.

"Well our good friend Tom here says he doesn't mind towing us to his house," Dez said looking at Pam for a reaction. "He said we could stay the night at his place and first thing in the morning he'll take me to get the truck fixed."

"We don't have that kind of money to pay him for all that," Pam expressed with a defeated look on her face. "Maybe this road trip wasn't a good idea after all."

18

"He said we can stay the night at his place and he'll fix our truck first thing in the morning; free of charge," Dez smiled. "I told him I had to talk it over with you first."

"Nah, nah, nah," Trina hissed from the back seat. "I ain't staying the night in the middle of nowhere with no motherfucking crackers!"

"Trina!" Pam barked. "Watch your mouth!"

"We don't know this white man from a hole in the wall," Trina said seriously. "Besides he looks scary, like one of them crackers from out of a scary movie."

Even though it wasn't right, Pam couldn't help but laugh. Her daughter was very outspoken and didn't sugar coat or water down what came out of her mouth. After giving the big white man a quick once over Pam had to admit the big white man did look a little intimidating and scary looking. "You are the head of this house hold, so whatever you suggest is fine with me," Pam announced kissing Dez on his wet cheek. She loved her husband and would walk with him through fire if she had to.

"I don't think it's a good idea," Trina hissed from the back seat. "I mean, we don't even have a clue where we are right now."

"At the moment we're stranded," Dez spoke in a calm tone. "And right now we don't have much of a choice."

"I guess one night won't be too bad," Pam said.

"Alright fuck it. It is what it is," Dez said as he stepped back out into the rain. He quickly shook Tom's hand. "Me and my family have decided to take you up on your offer."

"Smart decision. Now let's get your truck hooked up to my truck so we can get out of this rain." Tom quickly jogged over to his tow-truck and pulled it around in front of the Explorer. Tom hopped out and he and Dez quickly hooked the Ford Explorer up to the back of his tow-truck.

Back inside the Explorer Pam, Trina and little Dezzy looked on as Dez and the big white man hooked the Explorer up to the back of the truck. Trina didn't know what it was about the big white man, but something about him didn't sit right with her. Something about him bothered her and made her feel uncomfortable. Something about him just wasn't right.

Dez walked back over to the Explorer and slid in the driver's seat. "Okay, here we go," he said forcing a smile on his face. He too was a little nervous about heading to a complete stranger's house in the middle of nowhere, but at the moment what other choice did he have?

"We're gonna be fine," Dez assured everyone as the tow-truck began to pull the Explorer back out onto the highway.

WHERE AM I?

An hour and twenty minutes had passed and the Barkley family was still being pulled by Tom and his tow truck. "I thought you said his house was only a few miles away?" Pam said with a suspicious raised eye brow. The tow truck had exited off the highway over thirty minutes ago. Now the tow truck was pulling the Explorer down a bunch of dark dirt roads out in the middle of nowhere.

"That's what he told me," Dez said in a neutral tone. He was a little nervous and worried about where Tom was taking them, but he couldn't let it show on his face for the sake of his family. If he began to panic, so would his entire family. So for the sake of his family he had to stay strong. "We should be arriving shortly."

"I hope so," Trina said sucking her teeth, not hiding her frustration and anger.

Twenty minutes later the tow truck pulled up in front of a nice size brick house. The house sat in the middle of nowhere. A dirt road and dark woods were the only things that could be linked to the house.

"Looks like we're here," Pam said looking at the brick house. It was something about the house that didn't sit right with her, but at the moment she just didn't know what it was.

"It's about time," Trina huffed from the back seat as everyone hopped out the Explorer. Tom quickly jogged to the front door and opened it so Dez and his family wouldn't get too wet. Once everyone was safely inside the house, Tom closed the door and locked it.

"Nice house you got here," Dez said looking around at the nicely furnished house. This was the type of house that Dez saw himself buying in the future when he got back on his feet.

"Thank you," Tom replied with a smile. "Are ya'll hungry?"

Before Dez could say no, Little Dezzy had already blurted out yes. Pam had packed a few sandwiches, some cookies, and a few juices for them to snack on while on the road.

"I'll have my wife cook us all a nice meal."

"No, that won't be necessary," Dez protested weakly. "We have a few sandwiches packed away. We wouldn't want to put your wife through any trouble."

"No trouble at all," Tom said as he called his wife. Seconds later a white woman with blonde hair and blue eyes who looked to be in her late thirties or early forties emerged from the steps with a smile on her face.

"This is my wife Ann. Ann this is the Barkley family," Tom announced. "I told them that you'd fix them a nice hot meal."

"That won't be necessary," Dez said. "You've already done enough for us."

"Don't be silly," Ann said cutting Dez off. "We don't usually get too much company around here, so whenever somebody does drop by I always cook and tonight won't be no different." Ann turned and faced Tom. "Tom, show them to the guest room while I start preparing dinner."

"The woman of the house has spoken." Tom chuckled as he showed Dez and his family to the guest room. The guest bedroom was huge. It had a bathroom inside the bedroom, a walk in closet, and two Queen size beds side by side one another just how they were set up at hotels.

"Y'all can take a shower and clean up. Then once y'all are done, meet me and my wife back at the kitchen table," Tom said smiling. "Like my wife said, we don't get too much company around here so we'd love to enjoy you all's company while y'all are here."

Dez extended his hand to Tom. "Thanks again for everything. Me and my family really appreciate it."

Tom smiled and shook Dez's hand. "Don't mention it." And like that he was gone.

"Damn. I thought he would never leave," Trina huffed as she flopped down on the bed.

"Be nice," Dez said.

"No! You be nice Dez," Trina shot back calling her father by his first name just to piss him off even further. She was mad that she was forced to come along for this stupid road trip. She was mad that their car had broken down in the middle of nowhere, and she was definitely mad that she had to stay the night in this creepy ass house along with a bunch of strangers, and what really made her mad was the fact that through all this she had to be in Dez's presence. Just as Trina saw Dez about to say something, she quickly tossed her ear phones in her ears as the sound of Young Jeezy filled her ears. "*All we do is smoke and fuck, smoke and fuck,*" she sang along with Young Jeezy bobbing her head to the tunes. Before Dez could even react, Pam quickly stepped in front of him and placed three soft kisses on his lips.

"Pay her no mind," Pam whispered. "Let's get cleaned up, eat, then go to the bed, and when we wake up tomorrow all this will be over."

"You better talk to that girl while I'm in the shower," Dez said walking towards the bathroom. "Cause the next time she start talking slick, I'm going in her mouth."

Pam smiled as she watched her husband disappear inside the bathroom. Seconds later the sound of water from the shower running could be heard. She loved her husband to death and was just happy that he was finally home where he belonged. Pam walked over to Trina and snatched the ear phones out of her ears.

"What?" Trina asked with an attitude.

"This nasty little attitude you got," Pam said with a pointed finger. "Get rid of it. Don't make me tell you again," she warned. "Dez is your father whether you like it or not. You may not like him, but you will respect him."

"I don't have a father," Trina said quickly. "Wanna know what Dez and Tom both have in common?" she continued without giving her mother a chance to answer. "They're both strangers to me," she said seriously.

"Your father loves you to death and you know that."

"How!?" Trina spat. "Instead of being home with his family taking care of his kids and his wife, he was out in the streets breaking into rich people's houses, but he loves me to death right?

Fuck outta here!" No matter what Pam said, Trina wasn't buying it. She just couldn't understand how someone could say they love someone, then go out and commit a crime that they knew would land them in jail for a long time. That just didn't make sense to her.

As Pam looked around she noticed that the guest bedroom they were in didn't have any windows. That seemed a little weird, but Pam paid it no mind and turned her attention back on Trina.

"For your information, your father was a wonderful provider and every crime he ever committed was for our benefit. Yes what your father was doing was wrong, but he was doing it for all the right reasons," Pam pointed out. "So for me, tone it down a little bit and lose that attitude you hear me?" Pam said. "You hear me?"

"Yes, I hear you," Trina said sucking her teeth.

Thirty minutes later Dez, Pam, Trina, and Little Dezzy sat downstairs at the dinner table along with Tom and his wife Ann.

"So Dez, tell me what are you and your family doing down here in our neck of the woods?" Ann asked curious. For dinner she had made baked chicken, mashed potatoes, and sweet corn.

"We were heading to Disney World."

Tom and Ann laughed loudly. "Y'all are a long way from Disney World," Ann smiled. "So tomorrow when my husband gets your truck back on the road will y'all go home or still head to Disney World?"

"Disney World," Pam answered quickly. "And thanks again for welcoming me and my family into your home. We really appreciate it."

"No, thank you," Ann smiled.

"Thanks for what?" Pam asked confused.

"Like I told you, me and my husband don't really get a lot of company, so when we do get company we like to welcome them into our world with open arms," Ann said looking over at Trina noticing that she'd only eaten the chicken on her plate. "What's wrong sweetie? Not that hungry are we?" She nodded towards the untouched corn and mashed potatoes that sat on Trina's plate. "Back in my day my mother used to make us sit at the table until our plates were clean," Ann said with her usual smile on her face.

24

"Well, this ain't back in the day and you damn sure ain't my mother," Trina said rolling her eyes. She didn't like Ann and badly wanted to slap that stupid ass smile off of her face.

"Trina!" Pam exploded. "To the guest room now!"

Trina sucked her teeth, rolled her eyes, pushed away from the table, and stomped off towards the guest bed room. Seconds later the sound of a door being slammed could be heard.

"I'm so sorry," Pam apologized. She couldn't believe Trina had just embarrassed her and the whole family like that.

"It's getting late," Dez said rising from his seat. "Please don't mind my daughter Trina. We've been on the road all day and I think we all need some rest," Dez said trying to make a joke out of the situation, but really deep down inside he was pissed off and wanted to whip Trina's ass. But that was something that he definitely couldn't do in the home of strangers. Besides Dez was real big on keeping him and his family's business private.

"Not a problem," Tom said shaking Dez's hand. "Get you some rest and first thing in the morning we'll head out to my shop and get that transmission of yours fixed."

"Again, I appreciate everything," Dez said as him, Pam and Dezzy headed down the hall towards the guest bedroom. When they entered the room Dez slowly walked up to Trina stopping in front of her. He looked down at her and spoke through clenched teeth. "If you ever embarrass me or my family like that again, I swear I'm going to mop the floor with your face you hear me?" Dez grabbed Trina's jaws firmly and applied pressure.

"Do you hear me?" Dez growled. Trina nodded her head up and down. When Dez released Trina's face she broke down into tears. Dez ignored Trina's tears and walked over to the light switch and hit the lights as everyone found a spot to lay down and sleep. Dez laid down and shut his eyes. He badly wanted to get this day over and done with so he could start the next one. Hopefully tomorrow would be a better day; a much better day.

RISE AND SHINE

D ez and his family slept peacefully until the sound of the bedroom door opening then slamming followed by the lights being turned on woke them up. Dez looked up and saw twelve big rough looking white men and one white woman surrounding the bed. The only two that Dez recognized were Tom and Ann and they all had mean looking scowls on their faces. They no longer wore nice warm friendly smiles.

"Tom?" Dez said sitting up with a nervous look on his face. He noticed that all twelve of the white men held a killing instrument in their hands. They held axes, knives, pitch forks, and sharp machetes. "What's going on?"

"You my friend are in some deep shit," Tom told him with fire dancing in his eyes. "You are on the white man's side of town and I'm going to teach you and your family just what happens when you get caught on the wrong side of town."

"Please," Pam pleaded. The fear that was on her face only made Tom want to kill them even more.

"Ann you're down with this too?" Dez asked hoping she would have a heart and persuade Tom and his crew to let them go.

"Shut the fuck up!" Ann snapped. She held a sharp shiny knife in her hand. "I'm tired of *you people* always complaining about something. You can't get jobs, can't get in good colleges, the white man always holding you back. I'm sick and tired of all the excuses and honestly I don't want to see another afro, Jeri curl, dread lock, high top fade, waves, and weave ever again!"

"Tom," Dez said looking the man in his eyes. "Man to man I have a family. Can you please let us off with a warning? Please? Me and my family would appreciate it. Please?"

"You and your family have been breathing the white man's air long enough!" Tom barked as he roughly snatched little Dezzy off the bed by his ankles.

"Nooo, help!" Little Dezzy screamed out in fear as he pulled the sheets off the bed as Tom dragged his body across the wood floor. Dez quickly hopped up off the bed and lunged towards Tom. Two of Tom's friends quickly tackled Dez down to the floor and began beating him with the wood part on the pitch forks. Pam thought about hopping up off the bed, but the sharp knife that Ann pointed in her direction made Pam quickly change her mind. All she could do was cry as she watched the mob of white men drag her only son out of the guest bedroom. Seconds later the sound of the door being locked from the outside could be heard followed by the sound of little Dezzy screaming at the top of his lungs. Dez quickly hopped up to his feet and ran towards the door trying his hardest to get it open. After pulling at the door knob for two minutes Dez put his back to the door and slid down until his butt touched the floor. He buried his face into his hands and cried his eyes out as he was forced to listen to his son being tortured.

IT'S NOT A GAME

Tom dragged little Dezzy out into the living room and sat him on a wooden chair that sat in the middle of the living room. Tom's buddies quickly tied and bound him down to the chair. Tom looked down at Little Dezzy with a disgusted look on his face. He turned and slapped the taste out of Dezzy's mouth.

"Look at me you little Nigglet," Tom ordered, using his hand to raise Little Dezzy chin forcing him to look up at him. "You do understand why this is happening to you right?" Tom took Dezzy's silence as ignorance and continued. "I'm doing you and the world a favor," he paused. "I'm saving you from doing life in prison and saving an innocent person from having to be mugged or killed by you. You know how *you people* do." He laughed loudly causing the rest of his buddies to join in.

"My Daddy's going to kill you," Little Dezzy said interrupting Tom and his buddies laughing session.

"Oh really?" Tom said with a sarcastic smile on his face. He loved the heart and courage that the young man before him showed, but just like all the other niggers he came across Little Dezzy had more brawn than brains. Tom gave his buddies a head nod and they chopped away at pieces of Little Dezzy's body with the sharp machetes. Little Dezzy howled out in pain as his fingers were removed from his hands and then his hands removed from his wrist. As Dezzy continued to howl in pain, Tom grabbed a canister of gasoline and splashed the toxic liquid all over Little Dezzy's body until he was drenched. A sick smile was plastered across Tom's face.

"Burn in hell with the rest of the scum." He struck a match and tossed it on top of Little Dezzy's head. Instantly his body became engulfed in bright orange flames. Little Dezzy screamed at the top of his little lungs while his body jerked as he struggled to free himself from the chair, but it was no use.

"What's the matter?" Tom laughed wickedly. "I thought you people like Bar-B-Que's?" Once Little Dezzy was dead and burnt to a crisp, Tom tossed a heavy blanket over Dezzy's body and quickly put the fire out before it spread throughout the house. Ann looked on from the side line with a huge smile on her face.

"I love you so much," she said and then kissed Tom on the lips. "Can we kill that little bitch with the nasty attitude and smart mouth next?"

"Patience my love," Tom quickly answered. "One by one we will dispose of all of them and if you are nice, I may even let you help."

***

Dez sat with his back pressed against the door and cried his eyes out as he heard Little Dezzy's screams get louder and louder. It all seemed like a sick dream, but the pain that shot through Dezzy's body from the beating he took by the hands of Tom's buddies plus Little Dezzy's screams reminded Dez just how real the situation really was. Finally Little Dezzy's screams came to a stop and then the smell of smoke and burnt flesh filled Dez's nostrils. At that very moment he knew that his son was officially dead and it was nothing he could do to bring him back.

"What are we gonna do?" Pam sobbed as the pregnant tears rolled down her cheeks. She couldn't believe that this was really happening. The whole point and purpose of the road trip was to help her family bond with one another and come closer. Never in a million years did she expect something like this to happen. Shit like this was only supposed to happen in the movies, not to her and her family.

"What did they do to my baby?" Pam cried as the smell of smoke filled her nostrils as well. She could only imagine what her son was going through right now.

"Fuck all this crying shit!" Trina stood to her feet. "We need to figure out what we gon do when them motherfuckers come back!"

"Watch your mouth!" Pam snapped.

"Fuck that!" Trina shot back. "One of us is next, so we need to come up with some type of plan."

"She's right," Dez said slowly rising to his feet. "One of us is next, so we have to be ready when they come back." He was mad at himself for not seeing this coming. Nobody was that nice and there were no windows in the guest bedroom to stop their victims from trying to escape. From how militant Tom and his buddies were, Dez could tell that this wasn't their first time doing this. Only sick, heartless, evil people would be able to do something like this. Tom and his buddies were just straight evil. They used race as the reason for their actions, but in all reality they were just plain evil and sick human beings.

"So, what's the plan?"

"Let me think!" Dez barked. His words came out louder than he intended for them to. "Sorry," he quickly apologized. Everyone in the room was frustrated, but in order for them to make it out of Tom's house alive they would have to stick together and work as a team. Trina searched the entire room looking for anything she could use as a weapon. She didn't know about her mother or Dez, but she wasn't trying to get killed and die like some animal with her throat slit. She searched the room high and low and came up empty. Tom and Ann had made sure that there wasn't anything in the room that could be used as a weapon against them. Trina realized that this was something that was well planned and brilliantly thought out. Right then and there Trina knew that the only way she and her family were going to survive this is if they would have to outsmart and out think Tom and his wife. The only problem with that was they were on Tom's turf, which gave him the upper hand.

"Our best bet is to try and escape when they come in here for the next one of us." This was the best plan Dez could come up with. What other choices did they have?

"Why?" Pam sobbed. "Why is this happening to us?"

"None of that matters," Dez said quickly. He could only imagine what Tom and his buddies had done to Little Dezzy. He just prayed that whatever they did, they just didn't kill him at the end of the day. Little Dezzy was still a child and a good kid at that.

"We don't know what time Tom and his buddies are coming back, so we gon have to take turns sleeping," Dez said looking from Pam to Trina.

"What are we going to use as weapons?" Pam asked innocently.

"These," Dez said holding up his fist. Fighting was the only option left. He knew him and two women wouldn't stand a chance against Tom and his buddies, but Dez planned on going down swinging. Dez could see the fear on Pam and Trina's face and at that very moment he knew he had to protect the two remaining women in his life.

"You think they killed Little Dezzy?" Trina asked what everyone was thinking.

"I hope not," Dez said in a defeated tone. He hated being in situations that he couldn't control. "All we can do is pray for the best and prepare for the worst."

With no windows in the room, it made it hard for Dez to tell what time it was. He didn't know if it were morning, noon, or night. After Tom snatched Little Dezzy up out of the guest bedroom, Dez, Pam, and Trina were on pins and needles waiting for the mob of white men to return. The question wasn't if they would return, but when they would return. Dez struggled to keep his eyes open as he looked over and saw both Pam and Trina sleeping side by side next to one another. The more he told himself that he had to stay awake and not go to sleep it seemed like the heavier his eye lids became. Dez stood to his feet, walked over towards the bathroom, and splashed a handful of water on his face as he stared back at his reflection in the mirror. He silently asked himself and God, why him? Why did he have to be put in what seemed like the most fucked up situations? Why did his life have to be so difficult? Why was the hand he was dealt so shitty?

As Dez sat staring in the mirror he heard the door burst open followed by several loud footsteps entering the room. Dez quickly stepped out of the bathroom with his fist balled up. "I'm telling y'all now!" Dez barked. "Leave me and my family alone!"

"Or else what?" Tom challenged. The cold stare that his eyes held told Dez that he seriously hated black people. Without thinking twice Dez charged one of Tom's buddies and snuffed him. The punch caused the white man to stumble backwards a little bit. Before Dez got a chance to follow up, four of Tom's buddies jumped on top of Dez beating him down to the floor and restrained him. Pam and Trina both held scared looks on their faces. Neither one of them knew who would be the next to go.

"You niggers never were too smart," Tom said with a disgusted look on his face looking down at Dez struggling to break free of his buddies who held him pinned down on the shiny wood floor. Tom's hand shot out in a flash and he grabbed a handful of Pam's hair roughly snatching her off the bed.

"Nooooo!" Pam screamed and kicked and clawed at the floor as Tom dragged her out of the room. "Please help me!" Pam yelled looking at Trina as her body skidded across the floor. Trina hopped up off the bed. Instantly one of Tom's buddies back slapped Trina down to the hard wood floor. Once Pam was removed from the room, Tom's buddies quickly exited the guest room locking the door from the outside.

"Fuck!" Dez yelled trying to rip the door knob handle off the door as he cried out loud like a baby. First his only son and now his wife had been dragged out of the room by Tom and his buddies. Only God knew what was going on out there on the other side of that door.

***

As Tom dragged Pam through the living room, she noticed her son Little Dezzy tied to a chair burnt to a crisp. Immediately Pam threw up all over her clothes. She looked up and noticed three empty chairs sitting next to Little Dezzy's chair. Tom roughly forced Pam down into the empty chair next to little Dezzy. He watched as his buddies tied and bound Pam down to the chair.

"Why are you doing this to us?" Pam sobbed in a light whisper. She didn't understand why or how someone could be so evil and cruel. "Why Tom? Why are you doing this to us? We are good people," she pleaded.

"The only thing you people are good at is killing your own people," Tom said in a serious and firm tone. "And that's taking too long so I figured me and my buddies would try to speed up the process."

"You don't want to do this."

"Yes, I do," Tom said seriously. All of Pam's tears had no effect on Tom. He could care less if she cried her eyes out. She was no better than all the other women that Tom had killed before her.

"If you have any kind of heart in your body you won't do this," Pam sniffed with her tearful eyes staring up at Tom. Her eyes were pleading and begging him not to hurt her.

"The devil doesn't have a heart," Tom said and then walked off. Minutes later he returned holding a chainsaw in his hands. Tom pulled the cord making the chainsaw come to life sounding like a motorcycle engine.

"Please Tom… Please don't do this," Pam begged giving one last attempt to save her life. Tom ignored Pam's plea and aimed the chainsaw at Pam's left ankle. Pam screamed at the top of her lungs as the chainsaw cut through her flesh and bone like a hot knife through butter sending blood splattering all over the place. Once that was done Tom went on to the next ankle and then he went up to her knee cap. All of Tom's buddies stood around with sick smiles on their faces. The sight of blood excited and turned them on. They all laughed and joked as the chainsaw ripped through Pam's limbs.

Blood splashed up in Tom's face while the chainsaw vibrated in his hands as it ripped and cut through Pam's torso chopping her body completely in half; leaving blood and guts all over the floor. Just because Pam was dead, Tom didn't stop there. He placed the chainsaw down on the center of Pam's neck removing her head from her shoulders and the rest of her body.

"Stupid black bitch!" Tom growled and then spat down on Pam's body parts that rested in a pile in the middle of the floor. "Two down and two more to go!!!"

KILL OR BE KILLED

The sound of a chainsaw motor revving followed by Pam's high pitch screams told Dez exactly what was going on, on the other side of the door. What killed him the most was that there was nothing he could do to help or protect his wife from the monsters that stood on the other side of the door. Dez looked at Trina who sat on the bed with a terrified look on her face. The look on her face told Dez that she didn't want nor was she ready to die, especially not like this. The more Trina heard her mother scream for her life, the more the tears flowed down her cheeks.

"I don't wanna die like this," Trina said out loud. "Not like this!" This wasn't how Trina saw her life playing out and she definitely didn't see her life ending like this.

"I'm not going to let you die," Dez said to her just above a whisper. He didn't know how he was going to keep Trina alive, but the one thing he did know was there was no way he could let Tom and his buddies kill him and his entire family. Trina already hated him for getting locked up and missing her entire youth. There was no way that he could let his daughter die like this even if he had to sacrifice his own life to save hers. If that was what he had to do, then so be it. Dez would trade his life for his daughter's life without even thinking twice. Now all he had to do was figure out a way to protect Trina from the mob of vicious white men that stood on the outside of the door.

"Just shut up!" Trina spat. She was tired of hearing Dez run his mouth about what he was going to do and how he was going to protect her when he couldn't even protect himself. "Don't say nothing else to me!"

Dez stood to his feet and looked down at his daughter. "I'm not going to let them hurt you. You got my word on that."

Trina sucked her teeth. "How you going to protect me when you couldn't even protect Mommy or Little Dezzy?"

"I don't know," Dez admitted. "But I promise you ..."

"Just don't say nothing else to me," Trina barked cutting Dez off. "I'm tired of you and all your empty promises." She hopped up off the bed, stormed inside the bathroom, and slammed the door behind her. Inside the bathroom Trina sat on top of the toilet seat and buried her head into her hands. She knew whenever Tom and his buddies decided to return she was more than likely going to be the next one to go. The sad part about the whole thing was there wasn't nothing Trina could do to stop the inevitable. The more Trina thought about it the more it made her cry. The fact that she would never see her mother or brother ever again is what hurt her the most. Now she was stuck with Dez, the last person she wanted to be with before it was her time to go and his face definitely wasn't the last face she wanted to see before she died. Ever since Dez came home from jail it seemed as if Trina's life was spiraling downhill and of course in her eyes it was all his fault. As Trina sat on top of the toilet seat she heard a light knock at the door.

"Go away," Trina shouted. "I don't have shit to say to you! I hate you!"

Dez turned the door knob and frowned when he found out that it was locked. "Open up. I need to talk to you."

"I said go away!"

"Yo, stop playing and open the door!" Dez barked. "We have to stick together. Two heads are better than one." Dez knew his daughter was mad, scared, and upset with him and more than likely she figured this was all his fault. All Dez wanted to do was make things right with his daughter, but Trina refused to let him in and continued to push him further away. "I think I found a way out," he announced. "But I need your help."

"You think I'm stupid or something?" Trina countered. "I've been without you all my life, so if I'm going to die just let me do that without you too just like I've been doing everything else!"

That last comment pushed Dez over the edge. He took a step back, then came forward with a strong kick that sent the fragile

36

door clean off the hinges. He walked up on Trina and roughly snatched her up by the collar of her shirt.

"You better not ever let me hear you talking like that again!" Dez growled. "I've loved you since the day I saw your mother struggle to push you out of her womb," he told her. "And I'm going to love you until the day you die and that day won't be today!"

Whether Trina believed him or not, he didn't care and whether she liked it or not she was going to hear the truth. "Every decision I've ever made in life was for my family and yes I did go to jail, but before I made that silly decision me and you were inseparable. I fed you, washed you, and read you bed time stories every night before you went to bed. You were my princess then and you are still my princess now, whether you like it or not," he said finally releasing Trina's shirt. Dez reached in his back pocket and removed a black wallet. "Look at this," he said handing her a picture.

Trina glanced down at the picture and rolled her eyes. The picture he held in his hand was a picture of her when she was two years old sitting on Dez's shoulders with a huge smile on her face.

Trina handed the picture back to Dez. "That was then and this is now," she hissed. "I'm a grown woman now."

"I don't care how grown you *think* you are. You was and will always be my princess," Dez said as he raised his hand up towards Trina's head and removed a bobby pin from her hair. "While you locked yourself in the bathroom I was looking at the lock on the bedroom door and I think I can pick it," he said heading over towards the bedroom door. Trina followed closely behind pulling up the rear. Dez kneeled down on one knee, bent the bobby pin into a weird angle, and stuck it inside the small key hole. Trina silently said a prayer as she stood back and watched Dez work his magic. Just by the look on his face Trina could tell that Dez was determined to pick that lock if it was the last thing he did.

Fifteen minutes had passed and just when Trina was about to lose faith in Dez she heard him say, "I got it!"

Dez looked over at his daughter and smirked. "I guess breaking into people's houses taught me a thing or two," he said with a nervous smile.

"I'm scared," Trina admitted in a frail whisper. She had so badly wanted Dez to get the door open, but now that it was open she didn't know what to do and was afraid of what was on the other side of that door. Every time somebody went out that door they never came back and Trina wasn't sure if that was a chance she was willing to take.

"I know you're scared baby, but you gotta be strong," Dez whispered. "If we don't get out of here we're as good as dead," he explained. "And I already told you I'm not going to let you die. Even if I have to sacrifice my own life to save yours." Dez meant every word he said and planned on doing everything in his power to back it up and keep his daughter alive.

Trina stopped Dez just as he was about to step out of the room. "No plan or nothing?"

"We going to run out the front door and never look back," Dez whispered as he noticed how nervous and scared Trina looked. "You can do this you hear me? Don't start freezing up on me now. We gon make it up out of here," he said leading the way out of the guest room and into the hallway. The first thing Dez noticed was that it was deadly quiet. The only sound that could be heard was the sound of the rain coming down hard outside. Dez and Trina tiptoed over towards the front door until Dez suddenly stopped in his tracks.

"What's wrong?" Trina asked nervously.

"I can't leave until I'm sure Mommy and Dezzy are dead," Dez replied. "What if they're still alive?"

"Dez don't be stupid. They're dead and you know it!" Trina said in a harsh whisper. "Let's get the fuck out of here before these racist crackers wake up!" From how dark it looked outside Trina figured it had to be around one or two o'clock in the morning.

"I can't leave without knowing for sure," Dez said. "There's the front door. Run down the dirt road and I'll catch up with you.

I promise," he told her. "I'm just going to scan the house real quick and then I'm out the door." It was no way Dez would be able to live with himself if he left that house without his wife and son if they were indeed still alive. So with no other choice he turned around.

"Wait up," Trina said catching up with Dez. She was scared to leave his side and thought it would be best if they stuck together. Dez tiptoed through the living room and saw one of Tom's buddies asleep on the couch snoring loudly.

The white man had to be around 6'7 and weigh anywhere from 260 to 280 pounds. Dez turned, looked at Trina, and placed his finger up to his lips. The last thing they needed was for the big white man to wake up. Dez stepped further into the living room and saw a body that resembled Little Dezzy's burnt to a crisp strapped down to a chair. Dez didn't want to think negatively but he was pretty sure that the body that was strapped down to the chair belonged to his son. On the floor next to the chair that the burnt body sat in, looked like what seemed to be a pile of chopped up body parts sitting in a pool of blood. Right at that very moment Dez begin silently praying that, that wasn't his wife in the pile.

"Please Jesus don't let that be my wife! Please," he said silently in his head. Dez and Trina kept moving making their way from the living room to the kitchen. As soon as Dez stepped into the kitchen his heart leapt up in his throat. On the kitchen counter sat Pam's severed head looking back at him. That was all the confirmation he needed. Now he and Trina could make their great escape. Now Dez's main focus was keeping his only remaining family member alive. Trina entered into the kitchen before Dez got a chance to stop her.

When Trina stepped in the kitchen and saw her mother's head on the countertop in a pool of blood she could no longer keep her food down. "Arrrgh!!!" She heaved as she threw up all over the kitchen floor.

"Hey!"

Trina's body jumped when she heard the big white man's voice boom as he rose up from the couch and headed towards the kitchen.

"How the fuck did you get out of that room?" The big white man huffed. With each step he was quickly closing the distance between him and Trina who stood frozen like a deer caught in headlights.

Dez quickly grabbed a sharp knife off the counter and placed his back against the wall and listened carefully as the big white man's footsteps got louder the closer he came towards the kitchen.

"I guess I'm going to have to teach you a lesson," the big white man's voice boomed as his hand shot out and gripped Trina by the throat.

Immediately Dez sprung from around the corner and plunged the knife in and out of the big white man's stomach repeatedly. The knife seemed to have little to no effect on the big man. The big white man wrapped two hands around Dez's throat as the two men went tussling throughout the kitchen making a ton of noise. Dez continued to stab the white man all up in his mid-section. Blood spilled all over his hand and wrist as he jammed the sharp knife in the big white man's stomach and twisted the handle. Finally the big white man released his grip from around Dez's throat and dropped down to his knees staring up at Dez with a how did this happen look in his eyes. Dez removed the knife from the big white man's stomach and pulled his hair back forcing the big man to look up at him.

"This is for my son!" Dez growled, and then viciously slid the knife across the big white man's throat. Trina looked on in horror as the big white man crumbled down to the floor with blood leaking from his throat like a faucet. This was the first time she had ever seen someone get murdered especially in such a violent and graphic fashion.

Dez looked up and saw Trina staring at him. Her expression was scared and shocked all at the same time. Before he could fix his lips to say something, he and Trina both heard movement coming from upstairs followed by several lights being turned on.

Dez knew all the commotion coming from him and the big white man scuffling throughout the kitchen had awakened Tom and the rest of his buddies.

"Come on, we gotta go!" Dez shouted as he grabbed Trina by the wrist and took off towards the front door. Dez snatched open the front door and him and Trina quickly ran out into the pouring rain. Dez had no idea where he was or where he was going, but he knew he had to get as far away from Tom and that house as possible. Dez and Trina stopped when they reached the dirt road. Dez knew if he and Trina ran straight down the dirt road, more than likely Tom and his buddies would easily be able to track them down especially with them being on foot while Tom and his buddies had access to vehicles.

"Come on!" Dez held on tightly to Trina's wrist as he led her out into the dark woods.

Tom, Ann, and all of his buddies stood in the kitchen staring down at the dead body that lay still in the middle of the floor. The dead white man was a close friend and fellow soldier to everyone in the kitchen. This was no longer a game. It had just gotten personal. Tom walked over to the front door that was left wide open and watched Dez and Trina run blindly into the woods.

"Looks like we got a live one on our hands," Tom said in a cold and aggressive tone. "Grab your flashlights and strap up. It's time to go hunting!"

SURVIVAL

Dez and Trina ran through the woods blindly. They had no idea where they were headed, but they knew if they wanted to stay alive that they had to make it to the other end of the woods without getting captured by Tom and his buddies.

"I can't!" Trina stopped resting her hands on her knees sucking in as much air as she could. "I'm tired. I can't run no more."

"Come on, we gotta keep moving." Dez looked over his shoulder and saw several flashlight beams not too far away. "Suck it up."

"Dez, I can't run anymore," Trina hissed. "And my feet hurt."

Dez looked down at Trina's bare feet covered in dirt, mud, and grit. Before they left the house he had told her not to wear them stupid ass high heels, but of course Trina thought she was grown and felt she didn't have to listen to anybody. Now here she stood in the middle of the woods complaining that her feet hurt.

Dez firmly grabbed Trina's wrist with one hand, and he had the bloody knife in the other as he pulled Trina along. If they were going to stay alive Trina would have to thug it out and keep her feet moving. Dez planned on keeping his daughter alive by any means necessary. Whatever he had to do, he would make sure it got done. The rain and cool night air didn't make things any easier for Dez and Trina. The wet mud made it even more difficult to run full speed. Not to mention every few steps they had to try and keep from slipping and falling. Dez and Trina kept on running until they reached a lake that separated them from the other side of the woods.

"Shit!" Dez cursed looking for another way out of the woods, while Trina took a quick breather. The longer Dez and Trina stood there looking for another way out of the woods, the louder and closer Tom and his buddies voices could be heard, which meant they were getting closer and closer.

"We gon have to cross the lake," Dez said looking over at Trina as the words left his lips. He knew that his daughter wouldn't be feeling or agree with the idea of them having to get in that dirty lake water.

"Fuck outta here!" Trina replied looking at Dez like he had lost his mind. If he thought for one second that she was getting in that lake water, he was officially crazy. "I ain't getting in that water!"

"We don't have no other choice," Dez told her. "If we move now we should make it to the other side in five to six minutes."

Trina looked out into the pitch black lake as the rain drops made little ruffles throughout the water. It was dark so Trina wouldn't be able to see what was or what wasn't in the water.

"Fuck that! I'd rather die, before I get in that water," Trina said looking at Dez. "It's probably snakes and all types of shit in that water. Fuck that, I ain't wit it!"

"Now ain't the time," Dez said sliding the knife down in his back pocket. "We getting in that water and we making it to the other side of this lake."

Trina looked at Dez like he was insane. The look on her face told Dez to go fuck himself. Dez sighed loudly as he grabbed Trina's thighs and scooped her up on his shoulders.

"No! Stop! Put me down!" Trina yelled pounding on Dez's back like a drum. Dez ignored Trina's rant and quickly entered the cold lake water. Dez took around twelve steps in the water, and then lowered Trina into the water.

"I'm not carrying ya big ass across this whole lake," he huffed as he grabbed Trina's wrist and pulled her along through the lake. Trina cursed Dez out as she closed her eyes and walked as fast as she could through the ice cold waist high water. With each step she took, she could feel things rubbing, sliding, and swimming across her bare feet.

"I hate you! I swear to God I hate you!" Trina repeated over and over again.

43

Dez ignored Trina as he continued to pull her through the lake. She could hate him all she wanted. Dez wasn't concerned with whether she liked him or not or whether or not they would ever be friends. His main concern was to get her out of this alive and make sure she stayed that way. Dez himself also felt several things swimming by and brushing past him, but he paid the underwater creatures no mind. His only focus was survival and by any means necessary.

Dez and Trina made it to the other side of the lake and immediately Trina let him have it.

"Get your fucking hands off of me!" she huffed. Jerking her arm free from Dez's grip. "Look at my clothes!" Trina barked looking down at her soiled clothes. "You know how much I paid for these!?"

"Fuck them stupid ass clothes," Dez spat. "You need to be thankful that you're still alive," he pointed out. He was getting sick and tired of Trina and her mouth and he was two seconds from putting a foot in her ass. Instead of going back and forth with Trina he grabbed a hold of her wrist as the two took off even further into the woods.

***

Tom led the way through the woods with a sharp machete in his hand. He kept a backup machete in the holster that rested on his hip. Tom owned a gun, but when he killed all of his victims, he liked to feel the life come out of them so to speak so he hardly ever shot any of his victims. He enjoyed inflicting pain on his victims. Seeing fear in their eyes before they died turned him on and the excited thrill of stabbing a man to death or chopping their head off was such a desire and an adrenalin rush for him. Tom led Ann and his buddies to the lake and without thinking twice he and his crew entered the cold lake water. They were marching through the water as if it was nothing. The further Tom made it through the lake the madder he became. He had underestimated Dez and that one slip up now had him and his buddies trooping through the waist high dirty water hunting Dez and his smart mouth teenage daughter. The look on Tom's face was the look of a mad man. In his eyes all black people were ignorant, broke, and worthless, so by Dez escaping from his house, it made him feel as if Dez had somehow outsmarted him and that was something Tom couldn't allow Dez to get away with. Tom, Ann, and his buddies reached the other side of the lake and before anyone took another step Tom made sure he had everyone's attention.

"From here we going to split up," he told his crew. "Let's corner these niggers and kill them," Tom said sternly looking at his soldiers. "And remember on this side of the lake there are all types of wild animals and shit running around. I've never been on this side of the lake before, so I'm not sure what to expect. Everybody just make sure y'all keep your eyes open and be careful," Tom said nodding towards the sign that was implanted in the grass that read *"Beware of Wild Animals"*.

"We splitting up in four groups of three," Tom announced. "It's twelve of us and only two of them. Let's go hunting!" he said as each group split up and entered the woods going after Dez and Trina. Tom, Ann, and another big white man who carried a sharp ax trucked through the woods with no nonsense looks plastered on all of their faces and sharp weapons glued to their hands.

"When we catch these niggers, can I kill that little smart mouth black bitch?" Ann asked with excitement all in her voice. The thought of killing Trina brought joy to her eyes and a smile on her face. She just hoped and prayed that none of the other groups found Dez and Trina first and got to have all the fun.

"I don't care what you do with the little black bitch. All I know is that Dez is mines," Tom said in a matter of fact tone. He knew Dez wasn't smart enough to know how to survive in the woods with no food or water, so he knew it would only be a matter of time before Dez and Trina were captured and killed. The rain continued to come down hard. Tom and his team paid the rain no mind. This was nothing new for them. Rain, sleet, or snow they carried out their missions. They were predators. They were human killing machines with a thirst for blood that badly needed to be quenched.

"We're getting close." Tom stopped, sniffed, and looked around. "I can smell them. I can smell the fear dripping off of them," he said with an angry scowl on his face. He and his crew continued on through the woods in pursuit of their prey.

MAKE IT WORK

Dez and Trina splashed through puddle after puddle. Dez knew Trina was tired, but in order for them to stay alive they had to keep moving. Rest and sleep wasn't an option right now. As the two ran blindly through the woods, Dez suddenly stopped dead in his tracks forcing Trina to stop as well.

"What happened?" Trina asked looking up at Dez breathing heavily. She was tired, but knew the risk of them stopping so for once she didn't complain. The plan was to get as far away from Tom and his crew as possible. "Why did we stop?"

Dez quickly raised his index finger up to his lips. "Shhh," he said looking out into the woods. "Over there in those bushes," he said nodding towards a pack of bushes that ruffled and swayed from side to side. "I just saw something run over in those bushes."

"Something like what?" Trina asked with a raised brow. She didn't do the pet, animal, or insect thing, so whatever was over in those bushes better be something that Dez could kill.

"It looked like a cat," Dez lied not wanting to scare Trina. What he really saw run through the bushes was something on four legs that was two times bigger than a pit-bull. He wasn't able to identify what type of animal it was, but the one thing Dez was able to tell was that whatever ran through the bushes looked vicious and dangerous and he was thankful that the animal hadn't spotted them.

"Come on, let's keep moving," Dez said as he removed the knife from his back pocket. When he had entered the woods, he didn't expect for wild animals to just be roaming around freely. Dez didn't know what time it was, but he knew it was in the wee hours of the morning. He also knew there was no way that Trina would be able to run for much longer, which meant he'd have to find them a place to crash for the night.

Trina ran at a steady pace barefoot through the woods. She kept her mouth shut knowing that arguing back and forth with Dez wasn't going to fix or help the situation. All she wanted to do was live to see another day. Trina figured that Dez didn't have a clue where he was going. She didn't like Dez, but she was now starting to trust him.

Dez stopped when he found a nice sized tree that looked like he would be able to climb it easily. "We gon have to climb up this tree."

"Why? What's up there?" Trina asked curiously looking up at the thick tree.

"You need to sleep," Dez said plain and simple.

"I'll be alright."

Dez ignored his daughter and began climbing up the tree. Once on a stable and secure branch, he reached back and pulled Trina up. Dez and Trina climbed up two more levels of the tree and got as comfortable as possible.

"Get you some rest," Dez said while removing his wet shirt from off his back and placing it over the top of Trina's head and the back of her shoulders, and then patting his shoulder. "Rest now cause in the morning we have to keep moving," Dez said as Trina rested her head on his shoulder.

"You can have your shirt back if you need it," Trina offered. She felt bad using Dez's shirt to keep her dry in the pouring down rain. It was already a little chilly outside and the rain wasn't making it no better. "I don't really need it."

"I'm good," Dez responded. "A little water ain't going to hurt me," he lied. The truth of the matter was, Dez was cold and the cold rain drops added to the madness. Goose bumps ran all up and down his arms from the chilled raindrops. "Get some rest."

"Thank you Dez," Trina whispered. The situation they were in was a fucked up one and Trina knew that more than likely her and Dez wouldn't make it out of the woods alive, so she figured the least she could do was show Dez a little respect before the inevitable happened. "So, how long have you had that picture of me and you in your wallet?" Trina asked just to make conversation.

"I've had that picture in my wallet ever since it was taken," Dez explained. "When I got locked up, I had your mother send that picture to me immediately. I looked at that picture every day for the past ten years and I prayed when I was released from prison that you would still be my sweet little princess waiting for me with open arms."

"I mean," Trina began. "If you loved me so much or as much as you say you did, then why did you go out and commit a crime that you knew would give you an asshole full of time? That doesn't make sense to me. All of these years while you were gone, I watched Mommy struggle to make ends meet, watched her struggle and scrape up money to send you packages and make sure we had everything we wanted for birthdays and Christmas, watched her struggle to keep the lights on and a roof over our heads, and I watched her do all of this without you. If you loved us and I mean really loved us, then you wouldn't have did what you did to get all that time."

Dez listened to every word his daughter spoke carefully before he responded. "Do you really want to know why I committed the crime I did?"

"Nah," Trina said flatly. "I really don't care. It doesn't matter now does it?" she said sarcastically.

Dez went on to explain why he did what he did anyway, whether Trina wanted to hear it or not. "Ten years ago, you were getting bullied and picked on in the local public school. Every day you came home from school crying, so your mother decided she wanted to put you in this fancy, expensive, private school that we couldn't afford and when I looked in your little tiny eyes it was no way that I could tell you no, so I went out and did what I had to do."

This was Trina's first time hearing the real story about why and how Dez had ended up in jail. After hearing the story she felt a little bad about the way she had been treating him, but it was too late to rewind the hands of time now. "It is what it is," Trina

49

hissed. Even after hearing the story about why Dez had done what he did she still felt the same way about him and told herself that when she had kids of her own she would never abandon them, leave them for a long period of time, or ever not be involved in their life no matter what.

Not too long after the two had finished talking Dez heard Trina lightly snoring. Dez smoothly draped his arm around Trina's neck and pulled her in closer to him as he watched her sleep. Even though he was stuck sitting in a tree soaking wet, this moment was one of the best moments of his life; a moment he would never forget. If Dez was to die right now, he would die with a smile on his face and a good feeling in his heart. As Dez sat up in the tree he heard all kinds of sounds emerging from out of the woods. The type of sounds he heard send shivers up his spine. Whatever was out there in the wilderness, Dez prayed that he and Trina wouldn't have to cross it or their path.

LET'S GET IT

The next morning Trina woke up in Dez's arms. She yawned and stretched looking up to find Dez wide awake. He did what he said and stayed up all night looking out for any signs of trouble.

"You didn't sleep?" Trina asked covering her mouth. She knew her breath smelled like shit and didn't want to violate Dez's nostrils.

"Somebody had to stay awake while sleeping beauty got her rest," Dez joked as him and Trina slowly made their way down the tree.

"So, what did I miss last night while I was sleep?"

"Three of Tom's buddies walked pass about four hours ago," Dez told her. "That's about it. Oh and I heard some wild ass noises coming from the woods," he paused. "I don't know what's out there, but whatever it is, it sounds angry and vicious. I think it might be mad that we're on its turf."

"What kind of animal did it sound like?" Trina asked curiously.

Dez shrugged. "I have no idea, but whatever it is, it sounds big." Dez reached down and picked up a nice sized stick. He quickly removed the knife from his back pocket and began sharpening both ends of the stick turning it into a sharp double headed spear.

"Here," he said handing the spear to Trina. Dez had spent ten years in prison and knew how to turn the smallest of things into a weapon. He and Trina had to protect themselves from Tom and his buddies and whatever else was out there in the woods.

Dez picked up another stick and made a spear for himself. As he held the spear in his hands, he thought about how he would use it without thinking twice. His mind was already programmed to either kill or be killed.

Dez and Trina kept it moving throughout the woods. Trina's feet were killing her. All the rocks, sticks, and other things that were scattered all over the ground assaulted her bare feet. She kept her mouth shut and kept it moving. For as long as her and Dez had been walking she figured they should be reaching the other side of the woods soon. Dez and Trina came to a halt when they reached another lake. The difference between this water and the first lake water was that it was now daylight and Dez and Trina could both see how dirty and filthy the brown colored water looked. It looked more like a swamp than a lake and immediately Trina's mind went back to last night when she felt several under water creatures swimming pass her and brushing pass her skin. The thought alone gave Trina chills.

"Don't give me that look," Dez told Trina. "Yes we are getting in that water and we going to make it to the other side safe and sound just like we did last night." He grabbed Trina's hand and led her towards the swamp until Trina suddenly stopped dead in her tracks.

"What?" Dez asked looking down at Trina.

"Look!" Trina pointed to the sign that was hidden next to a row of fluffy bushes. The sign read *"Beware of crocodiles! Enter at your own risk!"* in big bold letters.

"You see any crocodiles?" Dez asked looking over at Trina.

"You must be crazy if you think I'm getting in that dirty ass alligator infested water," Trina snapped. The only way she was getting in that water was over her dead body.

"Fuck!" Dez cursed loudly out of frustration. The swamp had put a dent in his escape route. With the swamp blocking his path to the other side of the woods Dez would now have to figure out a detour and another way to get him and Trina out of the woods. Dez's thoughts were interrupted when he heard a deep voice coming from behind him.

"Going somewhere?"

Dez and Trina quickly turned towards the voice only to see three big white men standing there with mean no nonsense looks on their faces. In their hands two of the men held machetes and one held a sharp pointy pitch fork. Dez pushed Trina over to the side out of harm's way. He then gripped his spear with a firm two handed grip, took a few steps forward and yelled, "Come on motherfuckers!" Immediately the three men surrounded Dez and began circling him like animals did their prey. Dez quickly faked like he was going to lunge at one of the white men and all three of them quickly jumped back. Instantly Dez realized that the white men weren't used to combat. Most of their victims never made it out the house, so this was all new to them. Dez on the other hand had just spent the last ten years in prison, so fighting, stabbing, slicing, and cutting people was like a second nature to him.

The first big white man lunged at Dez wildly swinging the machete at Dez's head trying to take it off. Dez ducked down as the machete cut through the air missing his head by inches. Dez ducked down and jabbed the spear into the white man's mid-section, pulled it out of the white man's stomach and plunged the spear up into his throat. The big white man choked and gargled on his own blood. He clawed at the spear and then collapsed down in the dirt.

Trina stood on the side line in shock. Watching Dez stab the big white man to death right before her eyes made her feel good inside. She wanted the white man to die a horrible death just like her mother and brother had died. And seeing Dez kill the big white man in cold blood got her hyped. "That's right Dez," she said cheering him on from the sidelines. "Kill them crackers!"

Dez pulled the bloody spear out of the dead white man's neck and turned towards the next man in line. The white man with the pitch fork stepped up next. He twirled the pitch fork in his hands as he inched in closer and closer. The look of determination mixed with fear was in his eyes. He had come too far to back down now. The white man glanced down at his dead comrade and before he could look up Dez was already in motion. He jammed his spear so far through the white man's chest that the point exited through his back. Before Dez could remove his spear from the white man's chest the last white man standing sliced his arm with his machete. Dez ignored the pain and blood that leaked from his arm and grabbed the white man's wrist and bent it back as far as he could. The big white man howled out in pain, dropped the machete down to the ground, and then punched Dez in the side of his head forcing him to release the grip he had on the white man's wrist.

The punch caused Dez to stumble backwards a few steps. Both men regrouped. Dez and the big white man squared off head to head. Dez landed a stiff jab in the middle of the white man's face causing his head to violently snap back. Dez followed up with a quick four piece left, right combination to the white man's head, then a quick powerful knee to the white man's gut forcing him to drop down to one knee.

Dez stood in place bouncing up and down on his tippy toes, waiting and watching the white man closely. He knew the big white man couldn't fuck with him when it came down to hand skills. The plan was for Dez to use his fast hands and speed to dissect the man that stood before him. The big white man yelled to the top of his lungs and ran full speed ahead charging Dez like a bull. He hit Dez like a middle linebacker as the two went crashing into the swamp water making a big loud splash.

"Shit!" Trina cursed from the side line when she saw Dez and the big white man crash into the filthy swamp water. Immediately her eyes shot to the **Beware of Crocodiles** sign, and then back to Dez and the big white man splashing and tussling in the water. Trina just prayed that all the splashing that they were doing didn't wake up the crocodiles.

The white man made it up to his feet first. He fired off four powerful punches that landed cleanly on Dez exposed face turning his once handsome face into a bloody mess.

"Get up you little bitch," he taunted while landing more hard blows to Dez's head and face. The big man wrapped his large hands around Dez's throat and began squeezing the life out of him

54

as he forcefully shoved his head under the filthy swamp water, choking and drowning him at the same time.

Trina sat on the sideline watching Dez take a hell of a beating. She wanted to help, but knew it wasn't much she could do against the big white man. When Trina saw the white man shove Dez's head under water she knew right then and there she had to do something to help Dez out. Trina's sweaty palms gripped the spear that she held tightly and headed towards the swamp. The big white man had his back toward her, so she figured she could creep up on the white man and shove the spear in his back to get him up off of Dez. Dez's head had been under water for about thirty seconds and Trina knew he wouldn't be able to hold his breath for so much longer. Trina's movement came to a halt when she spotted something long slowly gliding on top of the swamp water heading straight for Dez and the white man. Trina stood frozen with her mouth wide open. She had only seen shit like this on the Animal Planet channel. She wanted to scream to give Dez and the big white man a heads up, but at the moment she couldn't find her voice. Trina watched in horror as the crocodile leaped up in the air with his mouth wide open, grabbed the big white man's head with its sharp teeth, did a twirling 360 with the big white man's body hanging halfway out of its mouth, and then landed back in the water making a loud splash.

Dez sprung from under the water desperately filling his lungs with air. He coughed loudly and repeatedly as he slowly made his way out of the dirty swamp water. Dez made it out of the water then collapsed down on the ground. Neither he nor his body was used to this type of atmosphere or this type of combat.

"You alright?" Trina asked kneeling down by Dez's side. He had just saved both of their lives and Trina was thankful to still be alive and thankful that she wasn't out in the middle of the woods all by herself. If that would have been the case Trina knew she would have been dead a long time ago.

"I'm good," Dez lied. He felt like shit and not to mention his body was sore and ached all over. His clothes being soaking wet didn't help the situation either, but he didn't want to scare Trina or have her worried. It was bad enough that they were both stranded and being hunted like animals by a mob of ruthless killers. His daughter didn't need anything else to worry about. Dez slowly made it back up to his feet, spit on the ground, walked over to one of the dead white men, removed his spear from out of the dead man's chest, and then looked up at Trina. "We have to keep moving," he said as him and Trina made a left and headed through the woods in search of a way out.

"You weren't scared back there?" Trina asked glancing over at Dez. He had just finished going head up with three big white men and a crocodile and came out of that victorious and on top.

"A little bit," Dez said downplaying how scared he really was. The only time he had ever seen a crocodile was on T.V., but to see one up close and in person was a totally different experience. One that Dez hoped he'd never have to relive again. "You thought I was dead right?"

Trina chuckled. "I can't even lie, when I saw that crocodile creep up on you and that white guy, I thought it was a wrap!"

Dez and Trina laughed and joked about the near death experience as they continued their clueless hike through the woods. Both of their legs felt like they were going to fall off from the walking they had been doing, but they'd both rather walk until their legs fell off, than to cross paths with Tom and any of his buddies.

"I need to sit for a second," Trina said sitting down on an oversized rock.

She sat with her leg across her lap and began to massage the bottom of her dirty feet. The bottom of her feet were covered in dirt and dried up blood. Dez sat his spear down on the ground and sat across from Trina.

"Gimme," he said with his hands held out.

Trina looked down at her dirty feet and then back up at Dez. "You bugging," she said. She was embarrassed at how dirty her feet were. The bottom of her feet were pitch black and not to mention the odor coming from all the walking she had been doing on the wet ground was strong.

Dez sighed, then reached out and grabbed Trina's foot and began massaging it. He rubbed all over his daughter's foot like he couldn't see all the dirt and feel all the bruises and cuts that covered her foot.

"Ahh, that feels good," Trina said with her eyes closed as Dez massaged his daughter's foot. He felt sorry for her. No teenager should have to go through what Trina was going through; no teenager.

"Dez?"

"Yeah"

"Can I ask you something?" Trina asked with her eyes still closed.

"Anything"

"Do you honestly think we going to make it out of these woods alive?" Trina asked seriously.

Dez paused for a second giving himself time to think about his answer and then said, "Absolutely". He was speaking in faith, hoping for the best, but preparing for the worst. Any obstacles that were put before them, Dez planned on running straight through them full steam ahead.

"You really think we can kill Tom and all of his buddies on their turf and survive whatever is out here in these woods?" Trina asked looking in Dez's eyes letting him know that she had heard the loud strange noises coming from out in the woods. Trina may not of known what type or kind of animal it was, but from the sound of things she could tell that whatever it was, it was huge, vicious, and more than likely dangerous.

"Tom is a bitch," Dez spat taking Trina's other foot into his hands. "If we want to stay alive more than likely we going to have to kill Tom and all of his buddies." He paused and glanced over at Trina. "And if we plan on staying alive I'm going to need your help," he said with a raised eyebrow. He was asking Trina to kill, to take a human life, to off someone's on switch.

"I've never killed anyone before," she replied innocently looking down at the spear that sat close to her foot.

"I know you haven't. I'm asking can you?"

A devilish grin flashed on Trina's face. "Of course I can."

That's all Dez needed to hear. He knew there was no way that he'd be able to kill Tom and all his buddies by himself. If he planned on accomplishing the mission and staying alive he would need some help from his daughter. The only way he saw him and Trina staying alive and surviving all this madness would be if Trina got her hands dirty. "Come on we've rested long enough. We have to keep moving." Dez helped Trina to her feet as they continued their hike.

YOU CAN RUN, BUT YOU CAN'T HIDE

Tom trucked through the woods with a mean look posted on his face. All this cat and mouse shit was really starting to piss him off. He was ready to put an end to this game once and for all. The more he walked, the more cruel graphic thoughts on how he was going to kill Dez and Trina popped into his head. Tom, Ann, and one of his comrades came to a stop when they reached the swamp and found two dead bodies sprawled out across the ground. Tom reached down and touched one of his dead buddy's wounds and checked the temperature of the blood to see if the body had just been slumped or if it had been dead for a while.

"It's still warm," Tom answered as the trio made a left and headed through the woods. The dead man's blood being warm told Tom that Dez and Trina had to be close by and that excited Tom. He knew these woods like the back of his hands and he knew that this was the only way that Dez and Trina could have headed. This part of the woods was the section that Tom and his buddies usually dropped off all of their dead victims and let the wild life do what they please with the bodies. The only problem with that was all the wild animals were now used to the taste of human blood and that had Tom a little worried. Usually him and his buddies would just drop the bodies off then leave, but now here he was walking through the very same woods that he knew were infested with all types of wild animals; animals that could identify the taste of human blood. The only advantage that Tom had at the moment was he was familiar with the woods. At the moment he had home court advantage and planned on using it to his advantage.

"I got something good in mind for those two when we finally catch them." Ann said out the blue. Her wheels were turning. Sick, violent, and horrible thoughts clouded her mind and the sick thoughts brought a smile to her face. It made her only want to catch Dez and Trina even more.

"Be patient baby," Tom said in a cool tone. He too badly wanted to hurry up and catch the father and daughter and he knew that it would only be a matter of time before he and his buddies tracked them down. When he caught them, Tom definitely planned on making them pay for all the walking they were making him do. "They can't run forever."

"They can't be too far," Ann said as her eyes darted to the left towards the slightest sign of movement. "Over there!" she pointed. Up ahead to her left she had spotted Dez and Trina walking through the woods at a steady pace. Immediately Tom, Ann, and his buddy took off after Dez and Trina. Tom sprinted full speed through the woods like a track star. His enemies were finally in his line of vision and he didn't plan on losing them again.

"I got ya ass now," Tom said to himself while tightly gripping the machete he held in his hand.

***

"So, how did you and mom meet?" Since the two knew they had to walk until they found a way out of the woods, Trina figured why not start up a conversation with Dez. She really didn't want to talk to him, but since he was the only one around it was either talk to him or talk to herself, so talking to Dez it was.

"I met your mother at the supermarket," Dez replied with a smile as if he remembered it like it was yesterday. "I tried to cut in front of her in line at the register," he laughed. "I ain't never get cursed out so bad in my life."

Trina shook her head. "Mommy was about that life back in the day?"

"She cursed me out, made me get in line behind her, waited for me, and then made me carry her bags to her car," Dez told the

60

story. The more he recalled the events, the more it made him miss his beautiful wife.

"What happened after that?"

"After I placed all of her bags in the trunk she told me for getting her all worked up that I had to treat her to dinner," Dez smiled. "So I invited her to my apartment and cooked her the only meal I knew how to cook at the time, spaghetti."

"Yuck!"

"What you mean yuck!?" Dez turned looking at Trina like she was crazy. "You used to love my spaghetti."

"That was back when I didn't know any better," Trina sucked her teeth. "I'd rather let Tom and them catch me before I eat anything you cook."

"You talk that shit now," Dez said waving her off. "Bet if I sat a plate of spaghetti in front of you right now you would tear that shit up."

"I can't even front," Trina chuckled. "Right now I'd fuck some spaghetti up," she admitted as the two enjoyed a good laugh, a much needed laugh, and a laugh that kept both of them from crying. Their laughs were interrupted when Dez heard what sounded like footsteps and bushes and branches moving from a distance.

"Oh shit!" Dez yelled out in shock when he looked back and saw Tom, Ann, and another big white man running towards them full speed. Dez grabbed Trina's wrist as the two took off into a full sprint. Running for their lives, the fear of getting caught and being captured seemed to make both Dez and Trina's legs move even faster. Dez and Trina dodged large rocks, sticky bushes, and anything else that may have been able to slow them down. Dez desperately sucked air down into his lungs as he craved his neck to glance back and see how much of a head start he and Trina had on Tom and his buddies. Seeing that he and Trina had a good hundred foot head start, Dez thought it might be a good idea for him and Trina to split up. After giving the idea more thought he decided that the two of them splitting up wasn't a good idea. How would he protect his daughter if they were separated? How would he even know if she was alright and safe? As the two continued to run, out of nowhere a big white man ran out the bushes and roughly tackled Trina down to the ground as if she were a crash dummy. The big white man springing from the bushes caught Dez off guard. He looked on and watched as the back of Trina's head bounced off the ground like a basketball.

Dez trained his spear at the big white man that straddled Trina's waist when two more big country white boys sprung from behind a different set of bushes. Both men held sharp machetes in their hands. Dez looked at the two big white boys that stood in front of him with murderous intentions in their eyes, and then glanced back only to find out that Tom, Ann, and the other big white boy were quickly closing the distance between them.

Dez quickly faked like he was going to strike one of the two white boys with his spear causing both of them to retreat, taking a couple steps backwards. Once Dez had a little bit of a distance between him and his two attackers he smoothly snuck up on the white boy that straddled Trina. Dez held the handmade spear with two hands, raised it high above his head, then shoved it down through the white man's back with extreme force causing the spear to enter through his back and exit out his chest. Trina quickly scurried back up to her feet with a tight grip on her spear.

Dez's spear made a loud wet squishy sound as he snatched it out of the dead man's body. He quickly glanced over at Trina. "It's either them or us," was all that was said and all that needed to be said.

Trina had no other choice but to use the spear she held in her hand to defend herself. She wasn't a murderer or nothing like that, but this was definitely a time to kill. Trina followed Dez's lead and inched her way towards the two killers that stood in front of her blocking her path to freedom. Trina had made up her mind. She didn't want to die in a ditch out in the woods in the middle of nowhere. Before the four of them even got a chance to engage in combat something slowly emerging from out of the woods caused all four of them to stand frozen right where they stood in total fear and shock. Dez took a few slow steps backwards when he saw a pack of wolves slowly making their way towards him, Trina, and the two big white boys hungrily licking their lips. Three wolves with shiny grey fur and sharp pointy teeth slowly began to circle the foursome. Dez glanced over at Trina and saw the silent tears flowing down her checks like a river. Dez didn't know too much about animals especially not wolves. He didn't know if they could sense or smell fear. He quickly grabbed Trina and moved her behind him shielding her as best he could.

"I'm about to run," Trina whispered nervously. She was scared shitless and scared for her life. If today did happen to be her last day on earth, she sure as hell didn't want to die getting eaten up by a pack of wild hungry wolves.

"Chill," Dez said in a tone barely above a whisper. It was four of them and only three wolves and as bad as he hated to admit it, he liked his chances. His thoughts were interrupted by the menacing sound of growling wolves.

"Come on motherfuckers!" one of the big white boys yelled at the wolves while taking a swipe at one of them with his machete. The first wolf lunged towards the brave white man. The white man swung his machete with two hands like it was a baseball bat. The machete cut through the air and hit the wolf across the face in mid-air chopping half of its face off. From there it was on. Dez and Trina both looked on as the last two remaining wolves attacked the two big white boys. The two men did their best to fight off the wolves, but it was no use because the wolves were too quick for the two white boys. The white men screamed out in pain as the wolves ripped, chewed, and ate through their flesh.

Both Dez and Trina looked on in horror as blood covered the wolves' mouth. They turned the two white men into breakfast, lunch, and dinner.

"Come on we gotta go," Dez said as him and Trina took off through the woods running full speed trying to put as much distance as they could between themselves and the wolves as possible.

***

Tom slowed down when he saw the wolves ripping two of his comrades into pieces. It wasn't nothing he could do at the moment that could help his two comrades. All he could do was watch as the wolves devoured the two men. Out of the corner of his eye, he spotted Dez and Trina running through the woods. God must have really been on their side because it seemed like Dez and Trina slipped out of every situation by the hairs on their chins.

"Now what?" Ann asked looking on as the wolves continued to pick at the two dead bodies. Dez and Trina were beginning to get on her nerves. She was ready to put an end to this chase and the urge to kill the father and daughter couple was at an all-time high.

"Patience," Tom said in an even tone. "We going to catch them," he said with confidence. The frustration posted on Tom's face was a reflection of Dez's ability to survive. Finally Tom had run into a black man that had a brain and knew how to use it especially under pressure and when it mattered the most. Dez's ability to use his brain was starting to piss Tom the fuck off though. In Tom's eyes there was no way that he would or could ever be outsmarted by a black man. A black man outsmarting him was just as bad as getting outsmarted by a child and that was something Tom couldn't and wouldn't allow to happen under no circumstances.

Tom waited ten minutes after the pack of wolves returned back into the woods before he led Ann and his buddy back out into the woods heading in the same direction he last saw Dez and Trina headed.

"It's time to stop playing with these niggers," Tom huffed with a serious look on his face.

NOW WHAT

"I need to rest for a second," Trina huffed while her full sprint slowed to a jog, and then she came to a complete stop and tried to suck up as much oxygen as she could. All this running was really starting to take a toll on her bare feet, not to mention this was the most running she did in a very long time. Trina's lungs were on fire and felt like if she took another step she would die from exhaustion. Thoughts of standing her ground and fighting until the death crossed her mind, but the thought of ending up getting burnt into a crisp like little Dezzy or chopped into little pieces like her mother was out of the question. Looking up at the sky noticing that the moon was on its way out which meant soon it would be pitch black out in the woods. In the woods, when it got dark was the last place Trina wanted to be.

"I know," Dez said looking around. Trina didn't even have to say nothing; he already knew what his daughter was thinking because he was thinking the same exact thing. "We have to find a spot to crash," Dez said looking around as his mind raced a hundred miles per hour. He didn't have a clue what he was going to do, but knew he had to do something. Five minutes later Dez helped Trina up into a nice solid looking tree. It wasn't much, but it was better than nothing and kept the two out of harm's way and away from all of the night life creatures that liked to roam through the woods at night.

"I'm starving," Trina whined. Her stomach growled loudly confirming what they both knew already.

"I'll find us something to eat tomorrow," Dez replied. He too was starving and hungry enough to eat anything. From the top of the tree Dez saw three of Tom's buddies searching for them through the woods with flashlights. They weren't on the right track, but they were a little too close for Dez's liking. Tom's buddies were invading his comfort zone and Dez didn't like it. He was too ready to just say fuck it and hold court right in the middle of the woods. The only thing stopping him was Trina, his main concern was her safety and wellbeing. "I promise!"

Trina sucked her teeth. "There you go wit that lying shit again!" If she did happen to make it out of the woods in one piece, the first thing Trina planned on doing was eating a nice big juicy steak with some French fries on the side and a vanilla milk shake.

"You know it ain't shit to eat out here in these woods, so stop it," Trina said with an attitude. Her hunger was making her cranky and a bit neurotic. She was ready to snap, but didn't feel like or have the energy to fuss, fight, or argue with Dez.

"Have some faith in your father for once," Dez told her.

"Father?" Trina echoed, and then chuckled. "Nigga please!" She looked over at Dez like he was crazy. "You just blew my shit!"

Dez shot Trina a murderous look. He so badly wanted to smack the shit out of her, but decided to take the more mature route and simply said, "Good night baby."

"I can't stand this nigga," Trina mumbled under her breath and rolled her eyes. She was trying her best to be nice to Dez, but it was just something about him that she just couldn't stand. In Trina's mind this whole ordeal was Dez's fault. If Dez would have stayed in jail where he belonged, none of this would have even been going on right now. If Dez would have stayed in jail Trina could have been eating that big juicy steak that she so badly craved right now instead of sitting up in some stupid ass tree looking and feeling like a jack ass. Right at that moment Trina made up her mind that she was done even speaking to Dez. Speaking to him was a complete waste of breath and definitely a waste of time.

"You alright over there?" Dez asked just trying to see if his daughter was alright. He knew they were in a fucked up situation and he knew Trina was hungry. He knew she would rather sleep in a nice warm bed instead of a tree and he also knew that the only way the two of them would make it out of the woods alive were if they stuck together.

"Yo my man, do me a favor," Trina said with an attitude. "Stop talking to me. You a bozo and I don't talk to Bozos," she said looking Dez up and down as if he was some type of peasant. "Matter of fact, tomorrow I'll go my way and you can go your own separate way. I'm sick and tired of you and your bullshit. Fuck outta here," she said in a dismissive manner.

"I'm sick and tired of your nasty attitude and smart ass mouth!" Dez barked grabbing the collar on the back of Trina's shirt. He roughly yanked her down the tree a few notches causing her to hang on to a branch for dear life. "You don't want my help no more? Alright well fuck you then! You can't stand to be around me right? Right?" he yelled. "Good! Get the fuck out of my sight before I hurt you!" he warned.

Trina made it down the tree and looked up at Dez with a pitiful look on her face. Her big mouth had finally got her into a world of shit. She wanted to be on her own and now she was.

"Where am I gonna go?" she yelled with tears in her eyes looking up at Dez who remained up in the tree. She didn't want to separate from Dez. She was just popping shit and letting off some steam or so she thought.

"You grown remember?" Dez reminded her. "And the last time I checked, grown folks took care of themselves."

"Fuck you!" Trina shouted. "Fuck you! I hate you! I didn't need you back then and I damn sure don't need you now!" She picked her spear up off the ground and then took off out into the dark woods alone.

"Shit!" Dez said to himself after everything was all said and done. He had lost his cool and now Trina was out in the woods in the middle of nowhere all alone. Dez was pissed off and upset with Trina, but at the end of the day she was still his daughter and that was something that would or could never change. The longer Dez sat up in the tree, the more he realized that letting her scurry off into the woods was a bad idea and a foolish move on his behalf. Dez sighed loudly as he slowly made his way down the

67

tree. He cursed himself out over and over again in his mind for letting his anger get the best of him. When Dez reached the ground, the first thing he did was grab a hold of his spear. The sounds he heard coming from out in the woods were unidentifiable and scary. He didn't know what was out in these woods, but he was sure he was getting ready to find out. Dez let out a deep breath, and then headed in the direction that Trina headed. He just hoped and prayed that she was alive and alright.

***

Trina walked timidly through the woods. Her head snapped from left to right at every little sound she heard. She didn't know where she was going or what was out there with her. The one thing she did know was that she wasn't out in the woods alone from all the different types of sounds and noises she heard. She knew someone or better yet something would be confronting her sooner than she liked. Trina hated that she had to be out in the woods at night time all by herself, but she hated and couldn't stand Dez. He just knew what buttons to push to irk Trina's nerves. She felt like if she stayed around him too long, his presence alone would just start to piss her off.

"Fuck him," Trina said under her breath as she continued to troop through the woods. She felt naked, alone, and helpless without Dez by her side. The truth was Trina knew she was dead wrong for running off at the mouth back there, but her foolish pride wouldn't allow her to admit that she was wrong and out of line; so instead she found herself without a pot to piss in or a window to throw it out of. Trina heard a ruffling sound of some bushes moving up ahead and froze in mid-stride. Whatever was up ahead, Trina prayed that it would stay right where it was. Trina stood frozen and afraid to move. She was scared to have the sound of leaves and loose branches crackle and crunch under her feet and notify whatever was out there of her whereabouts.

"Shit!" Trina cursed in her mind. Moments like this she wished that she wouldn't have parted ways with Dez. It was times

like this when he did come in handy. More aggressive ruffling sounds came from up ahead. The sounds almost caused Trina to shit her pants. The closer Trina looked, she saw a pair of eyes glowing in the dark. The bushes ruffled some more as the glowing eyes inched its way toward Trina causing her to take a few steps backwards with her spear pointed at the pair of glowing eyes.

"Come on motherfucker!" Trina mumbled ready to kill whatever was in the bushes. As Trina stood frozen in place watching what was watching her, the rain started to come down again. The creature ran out the bushes coming straight for Trina. Trina violently shoved her spear through the animal's body out of fear. She repeated this act over and over again until she was sure that whatever was trying to attack her was dead. When Trina finally looked down, her feet were covered in blood as she saw a dead boar lying in front of her with several holes in its body and blood everywhere.

"Stupid ass pig," Trina huffed looking down at the dead animal. "I'm the wrong one to be fucking with!" she yelled. Then she spat down on the boar's dead body. Trina was hyped up. This was her very first killing. The only good thing that came out of killing the boar was Trina knew if she had to do it again, she could.

"Yeah, you ain't gon talk shit now right? Yeah, that's what I -- -"

The sound of something growling behind Trina caused her heart to leap up in her throat. She was so shook that she couldn't even finish her sentence. Trina slowly turned around, looked down, and saw a hungry looking wolf staring at her licking its lips. The wolf's glowing eyes and wet silver fur made him look even more scary and vicious. The wolf growled again this time showing its pointy sharp teeth. The pigs blood that covered Trina's feet was beginning to get the wolf riled up.

"Easy boy," Trina whispered trying to talk to the wolf like it was a puppy as she slowly inched as far away from the wolf as possible. From the look in the wolf's eyes Trina could tell that he was hungry and she was looking like a Thanksgiving meal and dessert. "Stay," she whispered.

The wolf growled loudly, and then lunged towards Trina. Trina let out a loud scream and closed her eyes anticipating the pain that she was sure to come. Trina stood with her eyes closed when she heard the wolf let out a loud nasty sounding squeal followed by the sound of something getting slammed down hard to the ground. When Trina opened her eyes she saw Dez standing over the wolf violently stabbing the wolf to death with his spear. The wolf let out loud screams and cries before taking its last breath. Dez stood over the wolf looking like a mad man. Specs of blood covered his face and his shoulders rose then fell with each breath he took. Dez jabbed the spear down in the wolf's neck one last time for good measures just to make sure it was dead before turning to face Trina.

"You alright?"

Trina didn't reply; instead she ran into Dez's arms and gave him the biggest bear hug ever. At that moment she was just so happy to see him. If it wasn't for Dez, she would have been dead by now and right now she was happy and thankful to still be alive.

"Thank you! Thank you! Thank you!" Trina said over and over again. Dez didn't say a word; instead he just hugged his daughter and embraced her. This was the most affection he had gotten from his daughter since he came home and he didn't want the moment to end. Dez hugged Trina tightly and as the two rocked back and forth for a while Trina cried her eyes out with her head buried into Dez's chest.

"Thank you so much," Trina said again in between sobs.

"Shhh," Dez whispered down into Trina's ear. "We going to be alright," he assured her. Dez led Trina back towards the tree they had rested in earlier. It was late and he knew Trina could use the rest. Ever since they had escaped from Tom's house, the two had been on their feet non-stop. As Dez led the way through the woods, he listened to Trina cry and sob all the way until they made it back to the tree that they would be resting in for the night.

"You alright?"

Trina nodded, and then proceeded to climb up the tree. After the way she had talked to and treated Dez she was ashamed to even face him. The short walk through the dark woods gave Trina enough time to realize that how she had been acting towards Dez and treating him was unacceptable and downright ugly.

"Sorry again for all the mean and nasty things I---"

"That shit ain't about nothing," Dez said quickly cutting Trina off. He wasn't the type to dwell on or stretch a situation, especially a negative one. It was what it was, was his mind frame and attitude. "All that matters to me is that you're still alive and in one piece."

"Why?" Trina asked confused.

"Why what?"

"Why are you so nice to me?"

Trina turned to face Dez. "And I don't wanna hear that cause I'm your daughter shit either. I want the truth," she demanded.

"I'm nice to you because I love you and you are the only family I have left," Dez said with a lot of emotion in his voice. "I let my wife and son die." He took a second to regain his composure before continuing. "And I'll be damned if I sit back and let you die on me to. Over my dead body!"

"Thank you!"

"For what?"

"For loving me the way you do and as much as you do," Trina said sincerely extending her fist out to Dez. Dez smiled and gave her a fist bump.

"I love you," Dez told her.

"I know you do," Trina replied quickly. "Did you see how I handled that boar back there?" she said quickly changing the subject. Love was a touchy subject for her and a subject she really didn't want to discuss Dez.

Dez peeped how Trina swiftly tried to change the subject, but he played along. "Yeah, that was good work back there. I was impressed," he said with a wink.

71

"Yeah, you know I had to do what I had to do," Trina said as if she had killed plenty of times before. "I told that pig not to fuck with me," she said curling her arm making a small girly muscle.

"Check you the fuck out," Dez said as the two shared a laugh. This was the most Dez and Trina had talked since he had been released from jail. Usually the two were going at it, but this conversation was different. It was as if the two had a new found respect for one another. If Dez could have saved this moment for the rest of his life, he would have, but he knew after all the laughing and joking was over, the reality of them being stranded out in the middle of nowhere would set back in. "Nah, but all jokes aside that was some good work you put in back there."

"I did what I had to do," Trina said simply. "Thanks for coming back for me back there. I appreciate it."

"Don't mention it," Dez said waving her off. "That wolf had you shook though," he joked, nudging Trina with his elbow.

"I wasn't shook," Trina lied. "The wolf just caught me off guard. If I would have ran into that wolf head up, I promise it would have been a totally different---"

Dez quickly reached over and clamped his hand down over Trina's mouth. Down beneath them Dez heard movement followed by voices. There were three different voices if he heard correctly. Dez placed a hushed finger up to his lips signaling for Trina to be quiet as he pointed down below them. When Dez removed his hand from Trina's mouth the first thing she did was look down.

Down beneath them stood Tom, Ann, and one of his buddies. In Tom's hand he held a stick that had some type of cloth wrapped around the top. The cloth had large blue and orange bright flames bouncing off of it; turning the stick into a homemade torch.

"These motherfuckers are around here somewhere," Tom declared. He had a murderous scowl etched on his face. The cold rain drops bouncing down off the top of his head only seemed to add to his anger and piss him off even more. Tom had heard a woman's scream not too far away so he knew Trina had to be close by. The hide and seek game that Dez and Trina were playing was only making things worse. The longer Tom had to search for the two, the longer he planned on torturing them. They had no idea.

"No way they're still on the move," Ann said aloud. "They had to find a place to rest and wherever they are, they're close. Real close; I can feel it!"

***

Dez and Trina were trying to be as quiet as possible with Tom, Ann, and his buddy down below. For some strange reason Tom and his crew had stopped directly under the tree that they were hiding in. Dez silently prayed that Tom didn't look up because if he did he and Trina would surely be spotted and more than likely killed. Dez looked over at Trina and could see the fear in her eyes and the frightened *please don't let them spot us* look on her face. Dez winked letting her know that things would be alright; he hoped. Dez leaned over so he could whisper something in Trina's ear, but slipped and lost his footing in the process. He quickly grabbed a hold of the branch, but had to let go of his spear in order to hang on. Dez hung on for dear life not wanting the hard ground to be what broke his fall. Trina did her best to try and pull Dez back up to safety, but was having a hard time lifting Dez's grown man weight. After a few attempts Trina had finally gotten Dez back up in the tree safely. Once Dez was safely back in the tree the first thing he did was look down to see if the commotion had drew the attention of Tom and his crew. Dez looked down and saw Tom looking dead up at him. The two locked eyes and immediately Dez saw the eyes of a man with no soul. Right then and there he knew if he and Trina wanted to keep their lives they're only option was to fight.

TIL' DEATH

Tom stood looking around in deep thought. His mind was focused on finding Dez and Trina as quickly as possible. The faster he found them the faster he could have fun with them. Just as Tom was getting ready to continue his search he heard something falling from up above. A hand made spear that was made out of a stick landed inches away from his muddy combat boots. Out of reflexes Tom, Ann, and his buddy looked up and to their surprise there sat Dez and Trina sitting up in a tree with scared and nervous looks on their faces.

A smirk danced on Tom's lips. Finally he had caught Dez and Trina. He had them right where he wanted them. All the fun and games were over with. They were sitting ducks and had nowhere else to run. Tom looked over at his buddy and gave him a head nod. Immediately his henchman slid the machete he held down in his holster and proceeded to climb up the tree. Fuck all this waiting shit, Tom wanted Dez and Trina out of that tree by any means necessary and he didn't plan on stopping until the two niggers were nothing more than a memory.

Dez looked down and saw a big strong looking white man climbing up the tree at a quick and steady pace. The no nonsense look on the white man's face let Dez know that the man meant business and planned on playing for keeps.

"Yo," Dez said looking over at Trina. "We gon have to split up if you want to stay alive."

"What!" Trina spat looking at Dez like he was crazy. Splitting up wasn't a part of the plan. "No, I'm not leaving you."

"Listen!" Dez barked. "I'm going to distract them while you make a run for it," he told her. It wasn't much of a plan, but it was better than sitting around waiting to die.

"And go where?" We don't even know where the fuck we are right now," Trina pointed out. The reality of the situation was Trina was scared and afraid to be without or away from Dez out in the woods all by herself, especially with Tom and his vicious buddies lurking throughout the woods.

"Head back towards Tom's house," Dez said nervously looking to see how far Tom's henchman was up the tree. "Head back to the house and find the keys to one of the cars or the tow truck and go get some help. They'll never expect you to go back there."

"What about you?" Trina asked, with her voice full of concern. Dez couldn't tell if she was crying or if it was raindrops that streaked down her cheeks, but what he could tell was that Trina's feelings toward him were starting to change. He hated that the two had to part ways as soon as they were just beginning to get some type of a bond going.

"Don't worry about me. I'll be fine." Dez shot Trina a, *I got everything under control* smile. "You just make sure you bring some help for me."

"I got you," Trina replied, no longer able to hide the scared look on her face.

"If any animals or Tom's buddies cross your path, you make sure you do what you gotta do!" Dez nodded towards the spear in her hand. "You hear me?!"

Trina nodded her head yes. "I got you."

As soon as the words left her mouth, a hand shot out of nowhere and roughly grabbed a hold of her ankle causing her to let out a loud shocked scream. Trina looked down and saw the big white man trying to snatch her out of the tree. Dez quickly removed the knife from his back pocket and sliced the back of the white man's wrist, causing blood to spill out of his wrist like a water fountain. Even with an enormous amount of blood spilling from the white man's wrist he still held a firm strong grip on Trina's ankle. He fought and struggled to pull Trina out of the tree and hold himself up at the same time. The white man's eyes grew as big as saucers when he looked up and saw Dez standing over him holding a knife glittering from the moonlight shining from up above. In a swift motion Dez reached down and removed the big white man's machete from his holster. Dez stuck the knife back in his back pocket and stared down at the big white man with a murderous glare in his eyes. The white man fixed his mouth to say something, but Dez didn't give him a chance to get the words out. Dez gripped the machete with two hands, raised it above his head, and brought it down with force.

Trina screamed at the top of her lungs when she witnessed Dez chop the big white man's hand off at the wrist. Warm blood splashed across her face as she heard the white man fall out of the tree. She didn't see it, but heard his body hit the ground with force like he had been tossed off the roof of the empire state building. Trina looked down and noticed that the dead white man's hand was still tightly wrapped around her ankle. Dez quickly stepped in and removed the dead man's hand from Trina's ankle and tossed it over his shoulder as if it was a piece of random trash.

"I love you," Dez said and leaned down and kissed Trina on the cheek. "Get back to that house. Find the keys to the tow-truck and get us some help!" he said peeking down at Tom and Ann who stood down below. "Never forget how much I love you! Never forget!"

Trina got ready to reply, but her heart leaped up into her throat when she watched Dez turn and dive out of the tree as if he was jumping out of a plane.

"Oh my God!" she squealed as she rushed over towards the edge of the tree and looked down only to see Dez on top of Tom pounding away at his exposed face. "Watch out!" Trina yelled up from the trees as she watched Ann creep up on Dez from behind and jump on his back. "Shit!" Trina cursed as she held her spear and climbed down the tree as fast as she could. The thought of Tom and Ann killing Dez scared her, but at the same time she couldn't just sit around and watch Tom and Ann jump Dez and not help. She was from the streets and even though she didn't like Dez like that she refused to sit around and watch him get jumped. Especially not by some crackers. When Trina made it down to the ground level she looked and saw Dez fighting both Tom and Ann at the same time. She gripped her spear tightly and thought about turning the two on one into an even two on two fight, but stopped in mid-stride. Dez's words replayed over and over loudly in her head. *I'm going to distract them while you make a run for it. Get back to the house, find the keys to the tow truck, and get us some help.*

Trina stood there for a second as Dez's instructions continued to replay over and over in her brain before her legs began to run in the opposite direction from where Dez, Tom, and Ann were rumbling. *Get to that house.* Trina said silently to herself as she headed back in the direction she had just come from. *All I have to do is get back to that house and I'm good.*

GOD HELP ME

Tom looked on in horror as he watched Dez toss one of his good friends out of the tree. The white man's body floated through the air and then wind milled as it hit a couple of thick tree branches. The white man came down landing on his neck making a loud thud noise sounding like a sack of potatoes had fell out of a tenth floor window.

"Shit!" Tom cursed looking down at his one handed comrade. Tom and the dead man had a history and had known each other since kindergarten. This was no longer a racial matter. Dez had just crossed the line and turned it personal.

Tom spent another couple of seconds staring down at his childhood friend as the hard rain drops hit the ground causing mud to splash on the dead man's face.

"Baby, watch out!" Ann shouted, but it was a little too late. When Tom looked up he saw Dez flying through the air. All he had time to do was cover his head with his arms as Dez landed on Tom using him as a cushion to his landing.

Both men hit the ground hard and lost possession of their machetes in the rough and brutal landing. Dez quickly crawled on top of Tom, mounting him and began raining punches on his exposed face with both hands quickly turning Tom's once handsome face into a bloody mess. Once Dez's arms got tired, he reached for the knife in his back pocket, but before he could remove the knife Ann wildly jumped on his back screaming like a mad woman as she hit him on the top of his head and on the side of his face with a closed fist.

"Take your fucking nigger hands off of my husband!" Ann roared.

Dez reached back, then swiftly used all of his weight to lean forward and tossed Ann off of his back. Her body crashed down to the ground like a rag doll splashing in a puddle of dirty water. Dez raised his foot and brought the heel of his Nike boot down across Ann's nose breaking it. Before he could stomp her face even further into the mud, Dez felt a strong fist connect with the side of his head from his blind side. The impact from the punch caused Dez to stumble, but he didn't go down. Standing in front of Dez stood Tom. His body was muddy and the cold stare in his eyes screamed trouble. Tom's eyes quickly glanced down at Ann whose face was covered in blood, then back up at Dez who stood in a defensive stance ready to defend himself.

Dez had a chance to take off running, but decided to stay and stand his ground. He was sick and tired of all this running and hiding shit. If this was how his life was going to end at least he could go out like a man and not a coward. Tom stood in front of him crouched over looking like a heavy weight UFC fighter. Dez moved in and landed a jab that caused Tom's head to violently snap back. Before that Tom got a chance to recover a three punch combination to his head followed by a body shot causing his leg to buckle, but his pride wouldn't allow him to go down. There was no way Tom was going to sit around and let a black man whip his ass. He'd rather die before he lost to a black man at anything. Tom growled and charged Dez at full speed. Dez tried to side step and slip out of the big white man's way, but the wet muddy ground made it hard for Dez to get a good footing underneath him. Dez braced himself and let out a loud grunt as Tom plowed into him like a linebacker. Tom locked his arms around Dez's back, lifted him up off of his feet, and violently drove him down into a pile of mud. Both of their bodies slid several yards in the mud before coming to a stop. Tom and Dez both wrestled and battled for position. Each man was doing whatever they had to do in order to gain the upper hand. Tom made it up to his feet first and charged Dez throwing vicious elbow blows. Dez was able to block a few of the blows but not all of them. A hard elbow landed square on his jaw. Tom followed up with a series of straight right hands then finished Dez with a powerful upper cut that he threw from down at the hip. The punch dropped Dez face first to the ground. Dez crawled to his hands and knees, spit out a little bit of dirt and mud before a boot to his stomach left him in a fetal position.

By now Ann had finally made it back up to her feet. She got ready to jump into the fight and help her husband out, but the growling sound that came from behind her caused her to stand frozen in place. Whatever was behind Ann sounded so vicious that she was scared to turn around and see what threatened to attack the trio. Ann slowly turned around and what stood in front of her she couldn't even describe. The wild animal was bigger than a wolf, but a little bit smaller than a horse. At first guess Ann would say it was a panther, a black panther. This wasn't no panther. Whatever this was, it had sharp teeth that had to be at least eight inches in length. The beast eyes were red and glowed in the dark. His wet black fur made the beast look even more vicious, not to mention the saliva dripping from the beast mouth and teeth let the trio know that he was hungry and the three of them were looking like a full course meal. The bushes rattled and ruffled and out stepped two nice size wolves with hungry looks on their faces. The big black four leg beast took a few steps toward the trio flanked by the two wolves.

Ann slowly made her way back over to where Tom stood. She quickly handed him the ax in her hands that she intended to chop Dez's head off with, but that would have to wait until later. Right now they had a bigger problem on their hands. Ann slowly reached down and picked up one of the machetes from off the ground. She then took her foot and kicked the other machete over towards Dez. Dez may have been the enemy, but at the moment Ann and Tom could use all the help that they could get. They could get back to killing each other later. Right now it was man versus animal and from the looks of the type of animals they had to go up against, this wasn't going to be an easy battle.

"Nobody make any sudden movements," Tom ordered. "These wild animals react off of movement," he explained. "If we stay still we should be alright."

Dez wasn't used to being around wild animals. He was from the hood and his natural reflexes when an animal came around were to take off running. In the hood the biggest animal Dez had to worry about was a dog and even dogs scared him, so to be around two wolves and a huge beast that he couldn't even identify was like a nightmare.

Dez grabbed the machete and slowly made it back up to his feet. He took another look at the animals that they would have to go up against and without thinking twice he took off running.

"Fuck that!" Dez cursed. He sprinted through the woods running full speed. He could hear something chasing him from behind, but was too frightened to peek over his shoulder and see what it was. The wet ground and mud made it hard for Dez to run as fast as he really could. It seemed like the faster his legs moved, the slower he ran. Not to mention his wet clothes from all the rain that had been coming down helped slow him up. Finally building up enough courage to see what was behind him, Dez peeked over his shoulder and almost shitted on himself when he saw the big black beast quickly gaining chase on him.

Dez ran through the woods carrying his machete like he had the devil on his heels. The only thing on his mind was not getting caught by the beast. Dez breathed heavily as he passed several trees. He tried running in a zigzag formation hoping maybe that would slow the beast up a bit. Just as Dez got ready to cut to the left he felt a sharp pair of teeth bite down into his shoulder. The big black beast leaped in the air and bit down on Dez's shoulder tackling him to the ground in the process. Dez and the beast violently hit the ground with a loud thud as the two rolled, tumbled, and slid down a slippery muddy hill. This wasn't any old hill, this was a super steep hill. Dez and the black beast rocked and rolled for at least fifteen seconds before they reached the bottom of the hill with the big black beast landing on top of Dez. During the rough bumpy ride down the hill Dez lost control of his machete.

The beast still had his teeth clenched down into Dez's shoulder when they landed. He began violently shaking his neck back and forth trying to rip Dez's shoulder off in the process. Dez let out a sickening scream from the pain as he slipped his free hand down in his back pocket and removed the sharp kitchen knife. Without thinking twice Dez plunged the knife through the beast's throat repeatedly. Thick dark red warm blood spilled from the beast's neck and splashed all over Dez's face. The big beast let out a loud, awkward, and painful squeal but didn't release his grip from Dez's shoulder.

Once Dez saw that the knife to the throat wasn't working, he switched up his attack. The kitchen knife made a wet squishy sound when he pulled it out of the beast neck. Dez then took the knife and jabbed it down into the beast's eye all the way up to the handle. Immediately the beast released its grip on Dez's shoulder. Dez tightly gripped the handle of the knife that hung out of the beast's eye and gave it a strong turn. The beast collapsed down on its side and let out a deafening scream. Dez quickly switched positions and mounted the big black beast.

"You wanna fuck with me?!" he barked as he stabbed the big black beast repeatedly. Even after the beast was already dead, Dez still continued to stab away. "Huh? You must not know who you fucking with!" Dez hopped to his feet and looked around on the ground until he located his machete. He picked the machete up, stood over the big black beast, and brought the machete down on the beast neck repeatedly until the beast's big head was finally detached from his body. Dez picked the beast head up off the ground, dropped down to his knees, and looked up into the sky with his face still covered in blood. Dez let the raindrops practically wash away the blood as he looked up at the sky and let out a loud scream. Dez stood up and tossed the beast's head as far as he could. He picked up his machete and slid his knife back down into his pocket. Dez wanted to chill for a second and take a rest, but he couldn't. There was no way he could sit around when he knew his daughter was out there in the middle of nowhere all by herself. Dez took off in a light jog. There was no telling what else was out there lingering around in the woods that might want to use Trina as their next meal.

"Don't worry baby, I'm coming for you," Dez said aloud as he took off in the direction he had just left. Dez vowed to never leave his daughter's side ever again. No matter what.

RUNNING SCARED

After jogging for close to thirty minutes, Trina's lungs begged for a break. "Fuck this shit," she said with her chest rising and falling as she sucked up as much air as she could. Trina looked around and saw that night was turning into day. Her growling stomach reminded her that she hadn't eaten anything going on forty-eight hours and counting. It seemed like the more she tried not to think about food, the hungrier she became. Trina was not only hungry, but she was also super thirsty. Her throat was dry. She was parched and could badly use some fresh water. Trina found a nice rock and sat down. She looked down and the sight of her feet immediately disgusted her. They were bruised, bloody, and hurting like hell. Not to mention the smell of them almost made Trina's stomach turn. After sitting on the rock for a couple of minutes, Trina slid and sat down on the ground resting her back up against the rock. During the night she had heard several loud screams coming from somewhere out in the woods. She just hoped and prayed that the screams she heard weren't coming from or belonged to Dez. The way things had been going lately, Trina didn't know what to think or what to expect, so she did her best not to think about what was happening at the moment. To try and take her mind off of her horrible reality Trina tried to think about happy times. While Trina went down memory lane she accidently drifted off to sleep right there leaning up against the rock. She was so tired that at the moment the hard rock that she rested up against felt like a fluffy soft mattress leaving Trina exposed out in the open out in the middle of the woods.

***

"You alright baby?" Tom asked glancing over at his wife.

Ann looked down at the two dead wolves that rested not too far from her feet and nodded her head up and down. Half of one of the wolves' body lay on the ground in front of her, while the other half of his body lay a few yards away. The second wolf lay dead on the ground with his neck snapped backwards. Tom stood there holding a bloody ax in his right hand as blood trickled from his left forearm all the way down his wrist and hand where he had been bitten by one of the wolves.

"We have to get you back to the house so we can get that cleaned and bandaged," Ann said gingerly grabbing Tom's forearm so she could examine it. "Yeah, looks like he got you pretty good," she said as if she had been working in the medical field all of her life.

"I'll be alright," Tom said with a disgusted look on his face. Dez was truly beginning to piss him off. He had never wanted to kill a man as bad as he wanted to kill Dez. The fact that Dez seemed to keep being able to slip through the cracks is what really made Tom angry and want to kill Dez even more. But Tom knew he would have to make his way back to the house and get his arm bandaged up. All of the vicious animals out in the woods were used to and attracted to the smell of human blood from all the dead bodies Tom and his buddies had dumped out in those very same woods. Tom knew he was taking a risk following Dez and Trina out into the woods past the lake, but Dez had gotten so far up under his skin that Tom was at the point of no return.

"No," Ann said in a stern tone. "It'll only be a matter of time before these blood thirsty animals out here get a good whiff of your blood and turn us from hunters to the hunted."

"You're right," Tom said as he heard a sudden noise coming from his right. Tom gripped the ax he held with two hands and spun in the direction of the noise. He stopped in mid swing when he saw one of his close buddies that went by the name Jake standing there holding a sharp hatchet in each of his hands. Tom looked down and noticed that both of Jake's hatchets had blood on them.

85

"Where are the other two men I sent with you?" Tom asked curiously.

"They didn't make it," Jake said simply. "Ran into a few wild animals and," he paused for a second. "Let's just say things got a little messy if you know what I mean." He tried to tone it down out of respect for Ann.

Tom nodded his head in understanding. He knew firsthand how vicious the animals out in the woods were.

"What's the latest on Darky?" Jake asked as the trio began heading back towards the house.

Tom shrugged, "Last time I saw him he was being chased by a big creature that was unidentifiable."

"You think he's dead?"

"I hope not," Tom said. "That would take all the fun out of this whole thing, now wouldn't it?"

"I hope not either," Jack cosigned. He too was just like Tom and liked to inflict as much pain as possible on his victims. Jake stood 6'3 and weighed in at two and some change. He was rock solid and all muscle. Violence was his middle name and hurting people is what put a smile on his face and brought joy into his life. Nothing would make him happier than to find Dez and Trina and kill them with his bare hands.

As the trio hiked through the woods they made sure to keep their eyes open for any signs of wild life. The last thing they needed was to lose another soldier period. The plan was a simple one, to get back to the house, get Tom's arm bandaged up, and then head right back out continuing to search and hunt for Dez and Trina.

"What you plan on doing to these niggers when you catch them?" Jake asked with an evil smile on his face. He knew what ever Tom planned on doing to the pair of niggers would be something horrible, downright cruel, and he loved it.

"I'm going to break each and every single bone in their bodies one by one," Tom told him in a sickening tone. Just thinking about it made the palm of Tom's hands begin to itch.

86

"Look," Ann said in a hushed tone stopping in mid-stride and pointing out towards her left. "You gotta be shitting me." A big smile suddenly curled up on her lips. Over towards her left the trio spotted Trina sleeping peacefully with her back leaned up against a rock.

Tom quickly led the trio towards where Trina laid knocked out in a deep sleep. Tom, Jake, and Ann all stood over Trina looking down at her with victory in their eyes.

SLEEPING BEAUTY

Trina laid sleep out in the middle of the woods. In her dreams her, Pam, and Little Dezzy were having the best time of their lives at Six Flags hanging out, riding roller coasters, and eating cotton candy. The look on Pam and Little Dezzy's faces were priceless. The three of them just couldn't stop smiling. All throughout the dream Trina made sure she gave her mother and brother as many hugs as possible. The thought of losing them again disturbed her. Suddenly Trina was abruptly awoken by something wet splashing down on her face. Trina woke up gasping for air as if she was drowning.

"What the fuck!" she huffed when she looked up and saw Tom and another big white man standing over her with their penis's exposed peeing on her head and face.

Trina screamed as the warm urine assaulted her face, head, and hair. She tried to quickly hop up on her feet and take off running. Trina made it about six steps away before Jake violently clothes lined her. The impact and force was so powerful that it caused Trina to summersault through the air before hitting the ground like a ton of bricks. Trina laid flat on her back staring up at the sky trying to get her thoughts together and shake off the cob webs when Ann came out of nowhere and came down with a hard stomp to her face.

"Stupid black bitch!" Ann shouted kicking Trina in her ribs. For all the trouble and walking Trina and Dez had made them do, Ann was eager to make her pay. "Where's that nigger father of yours?" Ann shouted placing another kick to Trina's ribs.

The pain was intense, but still Trina kept her mouth shut.

Jake reached out, grabbed a handful of Trina's hair with much force, roughly snatched her up on her feet, and pinned her arms up above her head in a full nelson position.

Trina looked up and saw Tom standing in front of her holding a large hatchet in his hand and a no nonsense look on his face.

"Where's Dez?" His question was simple.

"Fuck you!" Trina spat bravely. She knew she was as good as dead. There was no way that Tom was going to let her live and she knew it. If Trina was going to die, she at least planned on dying with some dignity. Even if she did know Dez's whereabouts, she would never tell Tom. He would have to kill her first.

Tom's fist shot out in a flash and punched Trina in the pit of her stomach causing her to break out into a coughing fit. He then placed the sharp hatchet under Trina's shirt and brought his hand down quickly.

Trina stood held up in the full nelson position and watched as her shirt and bra fell down to the ground, exposing her young firm, round, and perky breasts.

"Now," Tom began. "I'm going to ask you one more time," he said looking Trina in her eyes. "Where's Dez?"

The look in Tom's eyes told Trina all she needed to know. If she didn't answer him he was surely going to kill her right where she stood. Tears streamed down Trina's face as she opened her mouth and replied. "Fuck you!"

Just as soon as the words left Trina's lips, she felt Tom drag the blade of the hatchet across her chest and stomach several times in a rapid succession slicing Trina up. When Tom got done with Trina, her chest and stomach looked like someone had played a game of tick-tack-toe on it. Trina howled in pain as she watched blood trickle down her chest and stomach. The cuts and slices were burning and stinging and that was just the beginning.

"Dez," Tom said still looking in Trina's eyes. "Where is he?"

Trina's eyes glanced down to the sharp hatchet that rested firmly in Tom's grip and then back up to this no nonsense look on his face.

"Fuck you!" she sobbed crying loudly like a baby. Trina closed her eyes and prepared herself for the pain that she knew was sure to come. She just prayed that her death would be a quick one.

Tom raised the hatchet in his hand and just as he got ready to bring it down he heard a voice yell out from behind him.

"You looking for me? I'm right here!" Dez said standing there holding a bloody machete in one hand and an extremely sharp kitchen knife in the other. The look on his face was also a no nonsense one. Dez and Tom locked eyes and like two warriors the two began walking towards the other ready to battle and fight it out till the death.

When Jake spotted Dez, he roughly tossed Trina down to the ground and joined Tom's side.

Trina looked up at Dez from the ground and mouthed the words, "thank you."

Dez winked at Trina and shot her a private look that said, "get up and run away from here as fast as you can."

Dez and Trina communicated with each other without speaking, but instead by facial expressions. Trina gave Dez a look that said, "what about you?"

Dez replied with a look that said, "I'll be fine. Now get up out of here; now!"

On a silent count of three Trina hopped to her feet and took off running. She headed back in the direction of the house.

Tom looked over at Jake and Ann with fire dancing in his eyes. "I'll take care of this trash by myself. Y'all go after the girl and I'll meet you both back at the house."

The look on Tom's face told Jake and Ann that the decision was non-negotiable and without further dialog Jake and Ann took off through the woods after Trina.

Once Jake and Ann were gone, Tom turned and faced Dez. Finally he was going to get the chance to kill the lucky nigger that went by the name Dez.

"Finally," Tom said with a smirk. He held the hatchet in a firm grip as he and Dez slowly inched closer towards each other. Neither man showed an ounce of fear, nor was backing down in their vocabulary.

Tom flinched at Dez, causing him to quickly jump back. Tom smiled as he leaned down in a low crunch preparing himself for combat. Dez never took his eyes off of Tom as the two flinched and jabbed at one another trying to figure each other out. It was either kill or be killed and both men planned on living to tell their story when it was all said and done. Tom tried to take a swipe at Dez's mid-section and with the reflexes of a cat, Dez quickly took a step back and sliced Tom on his already injured arm causing more blood to spill from the already open wound. If looks could kill, Dez would have been dead ten times by now. Tom ignored the burning and stinging pain in his arm and kept it coming. He didn't know the meaning of backing down. Tom went to charge Dez, but stopped mid-stride when he spotted something moving out the corner of his eye. Tom turned and saw a black bear come storming out of the woods heading directly for him.

The bear stood up on his hind legs and took a swing at Tom's head trying to take it off. Tom side stepped the bear's blow and chopped off his paw with the hatchet.

When Dez saw Tom engage with the bear, he quickly took off running trying to put as much distance between himself, Tom, and the big black bear as possible.

After Tom chopped the bear's paw off, he quickly took off after Dez refusing to let Dez out of his line of vision again. Tom heard the bear let out a deafening growl behind him. Before he could figure out what was happening he noticed two more bears appear out of nowhere running full speed after him and Dez.

"Oh shit!" Tom cursed loudly as he ran for his life through the woods. He breathed heavily as he kept Dez in his sight. He was pumping his arms as he ran making sure not to trip and fall over nothing in his path. One slip or mistake and that would be Tom's ass and he knew it. In the mist of running full speed, Tom glanced over his shoulder and noticed the two bears close on his heels. Behind the two bears Tom also spotted three silver coated wolves joining the chase closing the distance between them and him quickly. Tom glanced down at his bloody arm and realized that the smell of his blood is what was attracting all of the wild animals to him.

"Fuck!"

THERE WILL BE BLOOD

Dez ran full speed ducking and dodging tree branches, bushes, and rocks just to name a few things out in the woods that stood in his way. Dez was too scared to look behind him, but he could hear the footsteps of several animals closing the distance at a fast pace. Dez felt his body slowing down. He tried to will himself and his body to keep moving at its maximum speed, but it wasn't looking good.

"Come on Dez, you gotta push it," he told himself over and over again silently in his head. The last thing he wanted to do was die at the hands of a wild life animal in the woods out in the middle of nowhere.

"I can't run no more!" is what Dez's brain was telling him and his body was starting to oblige and slow down. His speed began to decrease slowly, but surely. As Dez ran his foot stepped on a man hole that was covered by a pile of leaves.

"Shit!" Dez squealed as he fell down into the hole. The manhole took Dez underground. The tunnel was pitch black and felt like he was on a water ride at a water park minus the raft. Dirty water and mud splashed on Dez's face as he continued sliding down the hole. He had to be sliding down the manhole at least fifty miles per hour. Dez's body jerked and turned with each curve. After about a two minute ride, Dez was spit out of the tunnel. He floated and glided through the air until he landed violently head first into a bank of warm water.

Underwater Dez slid the kitchen knife down in his back pocket, released the machete, and swam up to the top of the water. Dez's head popped up out of the water and he sucked in as much air as he could. His lungs were on fire and gladly accepted the oxygen. Dez frantically looked around trying to figure out just where he was when all that could be heard were loud squeaking sounds all around him. The more Dez looked around the more he began to make out where he was. From the looks of things he was in some kind of underground cave of some sort. It was dimly lit and scary looking. Just as Dez got ready to swim over towards the ledge that turned into a path, he felt something sting him in three different parts of his leg.

"Ouch!" Dez yelled looking down. Instantly his stomach leaped up into his throat when he looked around and saw what looked like a few thousand wet furry rats floating on top of the filthy water squeaking loudly. Dez hated mice, rats, and any other kinds of rodents with a passion. The nasty wet fur of the rats brushing up against him caused Dez's entire body to shiver as the hairs on the back of his neck immediately stood up. The loud squeaking sound of the thousands of rats that flooded the water attacked Dez's ears. There were so many rats in the water that they were starting to climb over one another.

"Arrrgg!" Dez huffed as he felt a few more stings as the rats took turns biting him all over. "Fuck!" Dez yelled loudly as he slowly began to swim over towards the ledge. With each stroke he took, he could feel several rats being moved with his hands. There were so many rats in the water that Dez had no choice but to swim through them. It seemed like the further he swam, the louder the squeaking became in his ear. Several rats rested on his back and shoulders as he continued on swimming towards the ledge. The sight of all of the wet furry rats disgusted Dez and made him want to throw up and rip his skin off. Dez reached the ledge and saw even more rats piled up on the ledge crawling all over each other looking wet, nasty, and squeaking loudly. He threw one hand up on the ledge, swiped away as many rats as he could, and pulled himself out of the water up onto the ledge. Once on the ledge, Dez walked through and kicked several nasty looking rats out of his path. He walked swiftly trying to get away from the rats. The ledge led to a dirt path that led to a dimly lit tunnel. Not having a lot of options, Dez slowly headed down the path that led down the dimly lit tunnel.

Tom could feel the bears and wolves gaining chase on him. One of the big black bears caught up to Tom and took a powerful swing at the back of his head. Just as the bear's huge paw was about to make contact with the back of Tom's head, he slipped and fell down the same manhole that Dez fell in.

Tom didn't know what was going on or where the manhole would lead him. He was just thankful to be out of the bears presence and still alive. Tom's body jerk and turned as he continued to slide down the dark tunnel picking up speed as the ride became a little more bumpy and slippery. After a two minute ride, Tom was spit out of the tunnel like a cannon. His body flipped and somersaulted through the air a couple of times before making a big splash in the warm bank of water. Ten seconds later, Tom's head popped up out the water. Immediately he spotted all of the rats. The underground cave was infested with nasty looking rats. Tom proceeded to swim through the rat infested water unfazed by the thousands of nasty smelling looking rats. At the moment the rats were the last and furthest thing on his mind. Tracking down and killing Dez was what was on his mind. Murder was at the top of his list and anything else wasn't important. Tom threw his hand up on the ledge and lifted his body up. Once on his feet, he violently stomped several of the rats as he followed the ledge until it turned into a path. This was the only way Dez could have gone. The cave wasn't small, but there weren't many places that one could go. During the bumpy and slippery ride down the manhole Tom lost his grip on his hatchet leaving him weaponless. Tom could care less about the hatchet though, now he would just have to use his hands as weapons. When it came down to hand to hand combat Tom was just as deadly with his hands if not more deadlier than a weapon.

Tom reached the path, looked down and saw a pair of footprints, and proceeded to follow them. He didn't know where Dez was headed, but his footsteps were sure to lead Tom straight

95

to him and when Tom finally caught up with Dez he had something real painful in store for him.

THE HUNTED

Trina ran blindly through the woods with a tired and scared look on her face. She wasn't sure what kind of animals were out in the woods, but from all the sounds she heard she could tell that whatever was out there was big and dangerous just from the sounds that she heard. Trina was officially all alone out in the middle of the woods. She hated that she had to leave Dez's side, but at the moment the odds were against them. Trina just hoped and prayed that Dez was okay and still alive. She may not have known a lot about Dez, but the one thing she realized in the short period of time of knowing him was that Dez was as brave and fearless as they came. Trina also realized that Dez would do anything for his family and that made her look at him in a totally different way. Now Trina wished that Dez was with her right now to protect her and keep her safe. The fact that Trina wasn't sure if she would make it out of the woods alive and in one piece is what made her being alone in the woods even scarier.

Trina's sprint turned into a light jog as her breathing began to get heavy and her legs began to get tired and slow down on her.

"Shit!" she huffed. She was tired, but she refused to stop. The last time she stopped to take a rest, she fell asleep and woke up in a full nelson and almost ended up losing her life. So, it was safe to say that her stopping to rest was out of the question. Trina's jog came to a halt when she reached what looked like a pond of some sort. Trina stood there for a second with a puzzled look on her face. She didn't remember seeing or crossing the pond and began to wonder if she was even going the right way. With time working against her, Trina stepped in the water that came up to her knees.

Once in the water Trina bent down, scooped up some water in her hands, and splashed it on her face trying to wash away the urine that stained her face, hair, and body. Once her face was clean, Trina continued on through the pond. At that moment she wished she had listened to Dez and changed her outfit and put on some sneakers because the gravel in the water was killing and taking a toll on her feet. As Trina walked through the knee high water she began to wonder and think about what she could use as a weapon in case she ran into Tom or any of his buddies. Her mind drew a blank. Right now all she could think about was getting out of the pond.

As Trina walked through the pond she jumped and screamed when she felt something brush by her ankle. She didn't see what it was that had brushed past her ankle, but her mind began to come up with over a million things that could have brushed past her ankle, causing her to immediately fear the worse. *"Fuck this shit,"* Trina said to herself as she began moving quickly through the water. Wild nature, animals, and under water creatures wasn't her thing. The faster she got out of the water, the faster she would feel much better. The sound of water splashing behind her caused Trina to turn in the direction of the noise with reflexes of a rattlesnake. Behind her Trina spotted Jake and Ann moving through the water at a quick pace with evil intentions in their eyes.

Trina took off running through the knee high water never looking back. Fear was making her legs pump ten times faster than normal. Her heart was beating a hundred miles per second as dry land came closer and closer with each powerful step she took causing water to splash all over the place. Trina glanced over her shoulder and saw that there was a nice little distance between she and her abductors. Her feet hit the dry land and she took off into the woods like a bat out of hell. Trina ducked and dodged low branches and pointy thorn bushes as she weaved and maneuvered throughout the woods doing her best not to let anything break her stride or slow her down. Getting caught by Jake and Ann wasn't an option. Trina was focused on staying alive and even more focused on making it back to the house. All she had to do was make it back to the house, find the keys to Tom's tow truck, and she would be on her way to safety and on her way to getting some much needed help.

Trina dashed through the woods like it was her backyard, barefoot and all. She knew firsthand what would happen to her if she was caught by Tom or one of his people. Flashes of Little Dezzy burnt to a crisp replayed through her mind followed by images of Pam's head detached from her body. Those images alone were nothing compared to what would happen to Trina if apprehended by Tom and his buddies.

Trina went to make a quick cut to her left, when her foot planted the wrong way. Trina heard a loud popping sound, yelled out in pain, collapsed down to the ground, and grabbed her ankle with two hands. She squirmed around on the ground in agony, wincing in pain, and yelling out a bunch of curse words at the top of her lungs.

"Oh my God! Oh my God! Oh my God!" Trina repeated over and over again as she hobbled back up on one foot. Trina's ankle wasn't broken, but she did sprain it pretty bad. Standing on one good leg, Trina half hopped and half limped moving as fast as she could. The fear of being captured was now even more intensified and terrifying than ever. Pain shot from Trina's ankle all the way up to her thigh with each step she took. The pain was so excruciating that the thought of giving up crossed Trina's mind until she came to the realization that if she did give up, her ankle wouldn't be the only thing in pain. The thought of staying alive and not ending up like Pam and Little Dezzy was the only thing that kept Trina moving.

Trina was only able to make it a few feet before she was roughly tackled and viciously slammed to the ground. Jake ran full speed and tackled Trina like she was a practice dummy. The blow knocked the wind out of Trina. The impact caused her head to bounce off the floor leaving her head pulsing like a heartbeat.

Before Trina even realized what was going on she felt a sized 14 boot come stomping down into her stomach, causing her to spit up some type of liquid or mucus as she began to cough violently.

"You and that nigger father of yours are really starting to piss me the fuck off!" Jake growled. This time he raised his size 14 boot and stomped Trina's head into the ground with no remorse.

"No matter how many of you niggers we kill, more and more of you just seem to keep on popping up," Jake said bringing his foot down on Trina's head again and again and again. By the time he got done stomping Trina out, her face was no longer recognizable. Especially with all the fresh blood that covered it.

Jake was about to leave Trina alone until he heard her whispering something from the ground. He squatted down so he'd be able to hear the little black bitch clearer.

"What you say bitch?" he yelled in her ear with a smirk on his face.

"I said you crackers can't break me, cause you ain't make me," Trina whispered flashing a bloody smile. If she was trying to piss Jake off even further, then she succeeded; especially with that last comment.

"You think that's funny?" Jake said aloud to no one in particular. "Okay!" He looked down at Trina's injured ankle and stomped on it.

"Arrrgg!" Trina screamed out in pain clutching her ankle. She had never experienced this much pain in her entire life and was surprised that she hadn't blacked out from the pain yet.

"Oh, what's wrong?" Jake smiled looking down at Trina on the ground squirming in pain. "You ain't gonna talk shit now right?" he barked as he bent down and punched Trina in the mouth.

Ann stood on the sideline with a huge smile etched on her face. Seeing Trina take a beating amused her and the thought of killing the teenage black girl excited her even more. The smell of Trina's blood spilling from her body caused Ann to lick her lips. She had been murdering black people with her husband for so long that the sight of one of her victims in a fetal position, bleeding, and begging for mercy turned her on.

Jake bent down and delivered another devastating punch to Trina's exposed face before standing straight up. He still wasn't done yet. Jake reached down and grabbed Trina's injured ankle and placed it in between his muscular arms like a headlock position.

Trina looked up at Jake with a bloody face and pleading eyes. "Please don't," she begged wanting the pain to stop. If Jake was going to kill her, she wished he would just do it and get it over with. "Please don't do this; please!"

Jake looked down at Trina as if she was speaking a foreign language that he didn't understand as he used all of his might and forcefully twisted Trina's ankle until he heard a loud snapping noise that let him know that he had successfully broken her ankle. Jake tossed Trina's leg back down to the ground and then turned and looked at Ann.

"Go ahead and get you some," he said removing the weapons from her hands so her hands would be free to put in work.

"Don't mind if I do," Ann replied with a smile. She reached down in her pocket and removed a pair of pliers. "I'm going to teach you what we do to runners," Ann said as she roughly grabbed Trina's wrist and slid her pinky finger in between the pliers. Ann squeezed down hard on the pliers and then twisted the pliers hard to the right until a snapping sound could be heard.

Right at that moment Trina passed out. Her body could no longer take or absorb any more pain, but that didn't stop Ann. She proceeded to break the remaining four fingers on Trina's hand with the pliers.

"That's enough," Ann said breathing heavily. "We'll finish her off once we get her back to the house. "I'm pretty sure Tom will have something special in mind for her."

Jake nodded in agreement. He removed plastic tie cuffs from his pocket and bound Trina's wrists together behind her back. Then he grabbed her by the ankles and dragged her through the woods back towards the house on her stomach.

IT'S DARK AND HELL IS HOT

Dez trucked through the cave at a fast, but cautious pace. It seemed like the further into the cave he walked, the darker the tunnel in the cave became and that wasn't good. As Dez moved through the cave, he saw and felt a few rats squeak and run across his feet. Compared to the amount of nasty rats he had just escaped, Dez liked his chances. Every time he heard or felt a rat run across his foot he jumped and made feminine noises. Dez hated rats so he wasn't ashamed about his reaction towards the rodents. As Dez continued to walk through the cave he heard movement coming from up ahead. He swiftly removed the kitchen knife from his back pocket and held it out in a firm grip.

"Who's there?" Dez called out as his voice echoed throughout the cave. No answer came back, but Dez knew for sure that he had heard movement up ahead. He figured it was some type of vicious wild animal of some sort, probably planning on turning him into their next feast.

As Dez inched his way through the dimly lit tunnel, he felt someone or something jump on his back. Next he felt arms lock around his neck as a choke hold was applied. Immediately Dez struggled to get whatever had jumped onto his back up off of him. Dez back peddled, ramming whatever was on his back into the wall. Their bodies bounced off the wall making a loud violent banging noise, followed by whatever was on Dez's back groaning and growling loudly. As Dez struggled to free himself of the choke hold, he felt a pair of teeth sink down into his shoulder.

"Arrrgg shit!" Dez screamed out in pain as he jabbed the kitchen knife over his shoulder into whatever was on his back. Instantly he felt blood spilling down his neck and the sound of a loud pain filled scream, then he was released from the choke hold.

Dez spun around and stabbed whatever had been on his back repeatedly until he was sure that whatever it was, it was dead.

"Motherfucker!" Dez huffed, breathing heavily as he stared down at what had been on his back. After further examination, Dez realized what had attacked him turned out to be a human. A scrawny skeleton looking black man lay dead before Dez's feet. The dead black man had on nothing but a pair of filthy superman briefs, along with over fifteen rat bite marks all over his skin. Dez figured that the black man was one of Tom's victims that had escaped from Tom and his buddies' murderous wrath. The black man must have figured Dez to be one of Tom's buddies and wound up losing his life due to the mistake.

Dez looked down at the dead black man that he had killed and began to feel bad. The black man's scrawny body told Dez that it had been a while since the man's last meal. Just as Dez was about to continue on through the cave, a sudden movement caused him to quickly turn to his left. Before Dez could figure out what was going on a nice sized rock hit him right between the eyes and the last thing Dez saw before he hit the ground was darkness. Dez was knocked out cold.

RISE AND SHINE

Trina was jolted awake as her face was roughly dragged over dirt, gravel, small sticks, leaves, acorns, and a few pine cones. Trina looked around frantically trying to figure out where it was she was at. When suddenly the pain kicked back in reminding her exactly where she was. Trina let out a loud shrill scream as she felt her body being dragged throughout the woods.

"Please! Please! Why are you doing this?" Trina cried loudly even though she knew her cries and pleases went on deaf ears. Maybe, just maybe her words may strike some type of core within the white couple who were dragging her to her final resting place.

"Please don't do this! I have my whole life ahead of me! If y'all have any kind of heart, then y'all won't do this!"

Jake and Anne both burst into laughter at the same time barely able to contain it.

"You heard that stupid ass bitch?" Anne nudged Jake with her elbow. "Talking about do we have hearts?"

"She's black, what did you expect?" Jake said as if Trina saying something stupid out of her mouth was expected just because of the color of her skin.

"I know if she don't shut the fuck up, I'm gonna go back there and give her another sleeping pill," Jake threatened. He was already pissed off bad enough and he didn't like or care for black people, so Trina's best bet would be to shut the fuck up and quit while she was ahead. Honestly Jake wanted to kill Trina right there in the middle of the woods, but he knew an act like that would certainly piss Tom off, so instead of killing Trina he planned on having a lot of *"fun"* with her. Then afterwards he planned on beating and torturing Trina inches away from her life. The thought alone gave Jake a hard on and cause little beads of sweat to form on his forehead. The closer to the house they got, the more Jake began to silently plan and visualize exactly what he was going to do to the teenage nigger bitch that he violently drug throughout the woods as if she was a piece of garbage. The more Jake thought about it, the faster he walked, and the bumpier and rougher Trina's ride became.

As Trina went along for the ride all she could do was say a silent prayer. If there was a God up in heaven she hoped that he heard her prayer and somehow sent an angel down to save her from the destruction that was sure to come.

***

Dez woke up from his involuntary nap and immediately found that his wrist had been bound together with his own belt. He looked up and saw a black woman with wild matted hair, wearing nothing but a filthy moldy looking bra and thong set standing over him holding a nice sized heavy looking rock up above her head looking like she was getting ready to drop the heavy rock down on Dez's head at any given moment.

"Please don't do this," Dez pleaded. "I'm not here to hurt you," he assured the woman with the wild hair.

"What are you doing here?" the scrawny woman said in a quite jittery tone eyeing Dez suspiciously. "Who sent you?"

"Nobody sent me," Dez replied quickly. "Please put down the rock. I'm fighting for my life just like you."

"Tom," the scrawny woman growled. "Where, where is he?" she asked with pain and hatred in her eyes. Dez could tell by all the scars and marks from being bitten by probably a million rats that Tom and his buddies had violated the woman and her family to the highest degree and now the woman planned on protecting herself by any means necessary even if it meant taking a life to save her own.

"I don't know," Dez replied. "Me and my daughter are stranded," he told the scrawny woman. "Tom and his buddies killed and slaughtered my entire family. All I'm trying to do is make it back to that house to make sure I can keep my daughter alive. Please help me!" His eyes begged and the look on his face said that he was sincere and meant every word he said.

The scrawny woman tossed the rock down to the ground then bent down and untied the belt from Dez's wrist freeing him of bondage.

"Sorry about that," the woman said tossing the kitchen knife that she removed from Dez's person down by his feet. "I thought you were one of them."

Dez stood fixing his belt as he eyed the woman that stood in front of him closely. After closer examination he saw that the scrawny woman was scared and afraid. From the looks of things it looked like she had been down here in this underground cave for a nice amount of time. By the look on her face Dez could tell that she expected him to save and rescue her, but boy was she sadly mistaken. Not only was Dez in the same boat as her, but he too didn't have a clue where he was or how or if there was even an exit or way out.

"No, I'm not one of them. I'm on your side," Dez told the woman. "Dez," he said as he extended his hand.

"Frankie," the scrawny woman replied with a firm handshake. "So what's your story? How did Tom catch you and your family?"

Dez gave Frankie the short version of how him and his family had gotten trapped off and ended up at Tom's house. Frankie then went on to explain how similar their situations were. She told Dez the stories of how horrible her family member's deaths were. Dez listened closely giving the stranger his undivided attention. He didn't speak, he just gave a nod here and there. It was obvious that Frankie had been holding in all of this and badly needed to get it off of her chest, so Dez lent her his ear. The more he listened to her story, the more he felt sorry for the stranger that went by the name Frankie. He still couldn't understand how Tom, his wife, and his buddies could do this to black people or any color people for that matter. Just the thought of it all made Dez sick to his stomach. The more he thought on the situation at hand the more murderous thoughts filled his mind. Each one was more and more graphic and violent than the one before. Each thought ending in the same pattern with Tom begging for his life right before Dez ended it abruptly making it as painful for Tom as possible.

"So," Frankie said. "You think we can find a way up out of here?" she asked looking around.

"We about to find out," Dez replied slipping the kitchen knife down in his back pocket. He then removed his T-shirt that used to be white once upon a time and handed it to Frankie. "Here put this on."

Frankie accepted the shirt and put it on. Instantly she didn't feel as naked or exposed as before. She flashed a dingy tooth smile from going days without brushing her teeth. "Thank you Dez," she said with the words coming from deep within her.

Dez replied with a wink. He stood still for a second trying to formulate some type of plan his head. All that was on his mind was getting up out of the cave as soon as possible so he could do his best to keep Trina alive. That's if she wasn't dead already.

"Come on," Dez said leading the way through the cave. He didn't have a clue where he was going, but he knew they couldn't stay idle for much longer. "How long have you been down here?"

Frankie shrugged.

"If you had to take a guess?"

Frankie looked up like she was in deep thought then said, "six or seven days give or take."

"Did you and your husband try to look for a way out of here?" Dez asked making small talk as the two strolled through the cave walking at a steady pace.

"I'm not married," Frankie corrected him. "That man you killed back there was my brother."

"Sorry," Dez said looking down at the ground. "I didn't mean to."

"It's okay," Frankie said quickly cutting Dez off. "It was a mistake. If I was in your shoes, I probably would've done the same thing."

And just like that the conversation was over and done with. Neither one wanting to elaborate further on the fucked up situation they were both trapped in. The both of them were officially stranded in the middle of nowhere. They were down in a cave with no one to turn to but each other.

"You said you had a daughter?"

Dez nodded.

"Where is she?" Frankie quickly covered her mouth with her hand. "Oh my God! Please don't tell me Tom has gotten to her!"

"Tom is somewhere down in this cave with us," Dez exclaimed. "As far as my daughter goes," Dez paused for a second trying not to get emotional. "She's out in the woods all by herself. The last time I saw her she was still alive."

Frankie placed a friendly hand on Dez's shoulder, looked him in his eyes and said, "I promise to help you get your daughter back alive if it's the last thing I do." At that very moment Dez could feel the hurt and sincerity in Frankie's voice and knew she meant every word that she spoke.

As Frankie walked her bare feet stepped in something that she assumed was mud, until her legs slowly began to sink into the mud as if someone was trying to pull her down to hell. "What the fuck?" she said in a somewhat confused tone looking down at her leg as it continued to sink further and further down into the mud. "Dez help!" Frankie cried out. "My leg is stuck!"

Dez looked down at Frankie's leg sinking down into the mud and the first thing that came to his mind was quicksand. He quickly stuck his arm out and grabbed a hold of Frankie's forearm and did his best to try and pull her up out of the quicksand, but he seemed to be having a tough time.

"Awww. It hurts!" Frankie screamed out in obvious pain. While Dez was pulling on her it felt as if something or someone was pulling her leg deeper into the quicksand like a tug-of-war was being played with her body.

Before Dez realized it, Frankie was waist level deep into the quicksand.

"Please get me out of here!" Frankie screamed in a panic tone. Her eyes were beginning to get wider and wider with each passing second.

Dez spread his legs apart, hunched over, used both hands, and slowly pulled Frankie out of the quicksand. As Dez watched Frankie's body edge out of the quicksand, he heard movement coming from behind him. Dez couldn't see who or what was behind him, but he knew whoever or whatever it was it had to be trouble.

"Come on! Come on!" Dez said in a hurried tone as he continued to slowly pull the remaining part of her body back on solid land. Once Frankie's entire body was back on solid land, Dez felt a powerful blow connect with the side of his head. The blow stumbled Dez, but somehow he kept his footing. He shook off the punch, looked up, and saw Tom standing there.

Tom stood there with a murderous look on his face. He looked down and saw Frankie on her hands and knees. He looked down at her hand that was close to him and stomped on it with the heel of his boot. Before Frankie got a chance to scream Tom grabbed the back of her head and viciously kneed her in the face.

From the amount of blood that poured out of Frankie's nose Dez knew that her nose was broken and from the looks of it, it looked to be a bad break.

Dez quickly charged Tom and once in striking distance, he swung hard wild haymakers. Tom weaved the blows and grabbed Dez in a bear hug. The two men fought and tussled for better positioning. Each man tossing the other against the wall. With Tom being the bigger man out of the two, he was easily man handling Dez with little effort.

Dez hung on for dear life and tried to fight back as best he could, but it was an uphill battle. Tom squeezed and did his best to try and crush Dez's spine in half. When he was done, the plan was for Dez to be rolling around in a wheelchair.

"Arrrgg!!!" Dez growled out in pain as he threw several rights and lefts to Tom's head. He then followed up with a few knees to Tom's mid-section. The blows had little to no effect on Tom. He took the blows well then began applying even more pressure to the bear hug. Just hearing Dez scream out in agony and pain made Tom apply even more pressure to Dez's spine.

Just as Dez thought his spine was about to snap in half, he saw Frankie creeping up on Tom from behind holding a nice size rock in her hands.

Frankie eased up on Tom from behind, raised the heavy stone above her head, and then brought it down with great force. The huge stone hit Tom on the side of his head dropping him instantly. Dez dropped out of Tom's grip onto one knee while he and Frankie looked on as blood spilled out of the gash that opened up on the side of Tom's head and leaked out mixing into the dirt and gravel.

Dez quickly removed the kitchen knife from his back pocket and then headed over towards Tom's unconscious body. He was ready to finally get this shit over and done with. Frankie stood blocking Dez's path denying him access to Tom.

"Fuck him," Frankie said planting both hands on the center of Dez's chest. "Let's figure out a way to get up out of here. The sooner we get out of here, the sooner we can find your daughter," she pointed out. "She is more important than this trash."

Dez thought about it for second. He badly wanted to slit Tom's throat and stab him 100 times, but what Frankie said was right. Every second they spent fooling around with Tom was time away from looking for and finding Trina who was left all alone out in the woods with the odds stacked up against her. Instead Dez picked up the huge rock and smashed it into Tom's face one last time. "Racist Motherfucker!" Dez growled looking down at Tom's rearranged face.

"Come on," Frankie said grabbing Dez by the hand leading him away from Tom's unconscious body that lay idle in the dirt. As the two walked off Frankie intertwined her fingers in between Dez's as they headed down the dimly lit dirt path. Both walked in silence caught up in their own thoughts. At that moment all they had were each other.

"Good looking for holding me down back there," Dez said out of nowhere. He was just grateful to still be alive and breathing and he had Frankie to thank for it. A total stranger that he didn't know from a hole in the wall had now saved his life not once but twice.

"Oh please," Frankie said waving Dez off. "You would have done the same for me," she said confidently. How could she not help Dez after he had just pulled her up out of a bank of quicksand? All she did was simply return the favor nothing more, nothing less.

"That was real brave of you," Dez commented. "You could've got yourself killed."

"You sound concerned," Frankie replied with a suspicious raised eyebrow.

Dez looked down and noticed that Frankie's fingers were still intertwined with his and he immediately released her hand from his grip. "All I was saying was thank you for saving my life back there." The more Dez looked at Frankie, the more he began looking at her in a way that he knew he shouldn't have been. He could tell that under different circumstances Frankie was a beauty that could probably stop traffic, if in the necessary attire.

Dez and Frankie stopped when they reached a fork in the road. "Left or right?" he asked.

Frankie shrugged. "Your guess is as good as mine."

Dez stood there for a long second trying to figure out if he and Frankie should go left or right. "Either get right or get left."

"We definitely ain't trying to get left." Frankie smiled as they headed towards the right path instead of the left. They didn't know where they were headed, but still walked in faith as if they had a map to the underground cave.

"So," Frankie said breaking the silence. "How old is your daughter?"

Dez sighed and shook his head. "She's only a teenager, but please don't tell her that." The two shared a soft laugh.

"I bet she's as sweet as pie."

"Hmmp!" Dez hummed. "Sho ain't!"

"Well I'm sure she loves her father to death."

"I wish," Dez thought to himself. No matter how Trina felt about him, Dez planned on doing all he could to keep her alive and

out of harm's way. Even if it meant killing Tom and all of his buddies.

Frankie picked up on Dez's short and quick reply to her statement and figured Dez and his daughter's relationship wasn't on the up and up. "Were y'all going through tough times?" Frankie asked.

Dez paused for a second and then said, "I've spent the last ten years in jail so I've missed a major part of her life and she's having a tough time adjusting to me being back around."

Frankie reached down and grabbed Dez's hand and squeezed it slightly. "You seem like a good man and a great father. Just give her some time to come around and I'm sure she'll see you for the good man that you are."

"If I didn't know any better I'd think that you were feeling me," Dez said with a whisk of a smile as he looked Frankie up and down.

Frankie blushed, ashamed that Dez had figured her out. "Honestly, I am feeling you a little something." She tried to downplay it, but it was obvious. "Any woman would be privileged to be with a man that will risk his own life to save hers."

"Like you said you would've did the same thing for me," Dez replied quickly. Frankie wasn't ugly or anything. She actually looked pretty good due to her circumstances, but that wasn't what was on Dez's mind right now. Right now his main focus was on finding a way up out of the cave and tracking down his daughter.

"What? I just want you to know that I appreciate what you did for me and thank you," Frankie said trying to keep it friendly. She had only known Dez for a short period of time, but already she could tell that he had a heart made of gold and his loyalty was one of his best qualities. Not to mention the way he loved his daughter was an even bigger turn on to Frankie. She could hear how much he loved Trina just by how he spoke about her and any man that took care of and loved his daughter as much as Dez did was good in Frankie's book.

112

Dez said nothing. The two continued the walk down the path hand-in-hand. Dez thought about slipping his hand from out of Frankie's grip, but decided to keep his hand put. If Frankie holding his hand made her feel safe, happy, and secure then Dez didn't have a problem with it.

Dez and Frankie came to a sudden halt as they heard movement coming from up ahead. From the sound of it, what laid ahead was something on four legs. Dez quickly pulled the kitchen knife from his back pocket and stood in front of Frankie blocking and shielding her from the danger that laid ahead. As Dez awaited what was to come he thought, *"maybe we should have went left instead of right after all."*

Seconds later Dez and Frankie both saw the beam of a flashlight.

"A rescue team maybe?" Frankie asked with her fingers crossed. She was praying for the best, but prepared for the worse.

"Doubt it," Dez whispered as him and Frankie stood on point waiting to see who, or what rounded the corner. The flashlight beam grew brighter by the second causing Dez's palm to begin to sweat compromising his grip on the handle of the kitchen knife.

A big white man emerged from the darkness wearing a pair of blue jeans, construction boots, and a red and black checkered lumberjack shirt. On his face was a mean looking scowl and in one hand he held a sharp knife that looked like it would be able to cut through a man's bones. In his other hand he held a leather leash and at the end of the leash stood a four foot tall K-9 with sharp looking teeth and pointy ears.

"Shit," Dez whispered as he quickly stepped into a shadow and pulled Frankie along with him. Deep down he hoped and prayed that the white man hadn't seen or spotted them, but when the flashlight shined on him and Frankie, Dez knew that they had been spotted and that the white man with the checkered shirt on definitely wasn't a part of no rescue team. He was a part of Tom's team of killers.

"Get em Sparky! Get em boy!" the white man barked in an excited tone as he released the leash and watched the K-9 run full speed off in Dez and Frankie's direction.

Dez watched in horror as the K-9 came running full speed, leapt up in the air, and viciously and brutally collided with and tackle Frankie down to the ground landing on top of her. The K-9 immediately went for Frankie's throat, but her survival skills quickly kicked in as her arms shot out in a stiff arm trying to keep the K-9's sharp and pointy teeth away from her neck. Frankie wrapped her hands around the K-9's neck struggling to keep the four legged animal from biting a hole in and taking a chunk out of her neck. The K-9 barked loudly and repeatedly as his face stood only inches away from Frankie's face. Nasty stringy saliva dripped and hung from the dog's mouth and fell on to Frankie's face. With all of her might she wildly bucked her midsection sending the K-9 airborne. The K-9 did a front flip and landed hard on his back. Within seconds he was already back on his feet charging Frankie. Frankie tried to make it back to her feet quickly, but she wasn't quick enough. She managed to make it to one knee when the K-9 lunged towards her. All Frankie had time to do was raise her arms and cover her face with her hands. The K-9 tackled Frankie back down to the ground and mounted her. Before Frankie got a chance to defend herself, she felt the sharp teeth of the K-9 sink down into her forearm.

"Arrrgg shit!" Frankie screamed frantically. "Get him off me! Arrrgg! Get him off me!" She continued to scream while her own warm blood splashed and dripped down her face covering it. The K-9 growled loudly as he viciously and violently shook his neck back and forth trying to rip Frankie's arm off in the process.

Dez heard Frankie's screams and saw the K-9 attacking her and blood everywhere. Just as he got ready to go help Frankie he saw the big white man with the checkered shirt charging towards him with the big shiny knife in his hand.

"Fuck!" Dez cursed as he planted his feet down into the dirt and gravel and prepared for the battle that was sure to come. He did his best to block out Frankie's screams and the K-9's rally behind him so he could focus on the killer that was closing in on him. Gravel and dirt flew with each step that the big white man took as he quickly closed the distance between him and Dez. Once within striking distance Dez landed a strong kick to the white man's goods. The kick was powerful, but didn't have a major effect on the white man. He took the kick well and still managed to catch Dez's leg in the process. The big white man lifted Dez's leg as high in the air as he could sending Dez crashing down, landing hard on unforgiving rocks and gravel. The hard fall caused Dez to lose possession of his knife. The man with the checkered shirt brought the knife he held in his hand down with force. His intentions were deadly and his swing was lightning fast. Dez caught the white man with the checkered shirts wrist in a two-handed grip in mid-swing just-in-time. Dez grunted and struggled with the white man that easily outweighed him by a hundred pounds as the glittering knife rested about an inch away from Dez's face. Dez's arm reached out and grabbed a handful of gravel from off the ground and tossed it in the white man's eyes temporarily blinding him. Dez quickly hopped up from off the ground and rained a combination of punches, elbows, and hard bone cracking knees to the white man's exposed face. Not long after the beat down the white man laid flat on his back unconscious. Still Dez continued to stomp the white man out until he finally got tired. Breathing heavily, Dez walked over to the corner and picked up a big jagged edged rock that looked to be the size of a cinder block. He walked back over and stood over the white man looking down at him with murder and hatred in his eyes. Dez slowly lifted and raised the big rock up over his head and held it there for a second as if he was contemplating on whether he should do it or not. Everything inside of Dez was telling him not to do it, but the more he thought about it, he kept telling himself that if the tables were turned the man with the checkered shirt wouldn't think twice about sparing him or Frankie's life so why should he?

Dez brought the rock down with force on the white man's face as hard as he could. His forehead quickly split open in a gash and begin to bleed. Dez brought the rock down again and another gash opened. His skin moved away from the bone on his head. Dez brought the rock down again, and again, and again until the man with the checkered shirts face looked like a pile of red applesauce.

Dez stood over the dead white man's body looking down at his handy work, until Frankie screamed and snapped him out of his zone. He immediately grabbed his knife from off the floor, turned, and headed towards Frankie and the K-9. Dez walked up on the K-9 from behind, reached underneath him, gripped the dog's family jewels, and chopped them off with a swift swing of the knife. Instantly the K-9 released Frankie's arm and let out a high pitch deafening howl that could wake up at dead. Dez dropped the knife down to the ground, grabbed the leather leash with a two-handed grip, and with all of his might he began spinning around and swinging the K-9 through the air by his neck. He spun around a few times, built up enough momentum, and released the leather leash sending the K-9 viciously slamming into the wall that was made out of stone. The K-9 hit the wall with great force, then dropped down to the floor with just as much force.

"You wanna bite motherfuckers right?" Dez said, speaking to no one in particular as he walked up to the injured K-9. He kneeled down and grabbed the dog's neck in a head lock. Dez twisted and snapped the K-9's neck killing him instantly. Just from the snapping sound that echoed throughout the cave, Dez knew the dog's neck had been broken probably in more places than one.

Dez stood there looking down at the dead K-9 for a second. It seemed the longer he stayed stranded, the more violent, vicious, and ruthless he was becoming and quite frankly he was beginning to like, enjoy, and maybe even love all of the killing. Something about killing all of the white men that killed his wife and son made Dez feel good inside. It made him feel a sense of accomplishment. If he was going down, he was glad that a few if not all of them would be going down with him whether they wanted to or not. The choice wasn't optional or negotiable. Just by looking at Dez's face one would have assumed that he wanted to spit on the dead K-9.

Frankie grunting in obvious pain caused Dez to break out of his thoughts and walk over and attend to Frankie and her wounds.

"You alright?" he asked lifting Frankie's arms so he could get a better look. "Not too bad."

"It hurts real badly," Frankie whined like a baby. She slowly made it back up to her feet as blood ran from her forearm down to the palm her hand.

"Come on we have to keep moving," Dez said leading the way down the path. *"There has to be a way out of here up ahead somewhere,"* Dez figured since the man with the checkered shirt and his dog had suddenly appeared in the cave coming from a whole different direction. Dez wasn't going to stop until him and Frankie found a way out of the cave. "You gon be alright or do we need to stop?"

"I'm good," Frankie said forcing a smile her face. "There is a beautiful young lady out there in the woods somewhere that needs our help. We can stop and take a rest later."

With that being said Dez and Frankie continued on down the path, hoping to stumble across a way out of the cave somehow. If there was a way out they weren't going to stop walking until they found it.

WELCOME TO HELL

Trina's skin felt like it was on fire after being dragged all throughout the woods. She wasn't sure how much more pain her body could take. After being dragged all throughout the woods Trina was beginning to lose hope. The thought of her getting saved or rescued seemed farfetched at the moment. She was left all alone in the woods with her abductors, left for dead, left to die a horrible death, and left to never be seen or heard from again. Trina's thoughts came to an end when she felt Jake lift her up and toss her over his shoulder like a sack of potatoes. He carried her through the very first lake that Trina and Dez had crossed when they had first entered the woods. Trina craned her neck and could see Tom's house from a distance through all of the trees. The closer and closer that they made it to the house the harder Trina cried. For the simple fact that she knew that once she was back inside the house she wouldn't be leaving alive.

Trina knew once they got inside the house she was going to die. She just hoped and prayed that it would be quick and not too painful. *"Haven't I already suffered enough?"* she thought silently as the smell from the dirty lake water made her stomach hurt. Her mind raced a hundred miles per second trying to figure out a way that she could escape from out of Jake and Ann's custody, but the more she looked around and the more her mind thought and tried to figure out and come up with a plan, the more her mind seemed to draw a blank.

Trina was tired mentally and physically. Her mouth was dry and felt like cotton, her body ached and was in tremendous pain, and after everything that went on, it still wasn't over yet.

As Trina rested on Jake's shoulder she could hear him and Ann laughing and joking about all the fun they were about to have with her. The sick and horrible things that Trina heard made her wish that she was already dead. No human being deserved this especially not a teenager.

Once Jake's feet touched dry land, he violently tossed Trina off his shoulder down to the hard ground. Trina hit the ground hard, let out a loud painful grunt, and winced as her already broken ankle landed awkwardly.

"Shut all that crying up!" Ann growled as she turned and hog spit on Trina. After all the running Dez and Trina made them do, they were sure to make her pay for all of their troubles. The closer they made it back to the house, the bigger the smile on Ann's face became. She couldn't wait for her husband to get home and see that she had did her part by catching and capturing Trina. Ann was sure that her husband would be beyond proud of her and everyone knew Ann lived to make her husband proud.

"If I was you, I would save those tears," Ann said chuckling. "Trust me when we get inside that house you're going to need them," she said in a matter of fact tone.

Trina ignored Ann as she felt Jake grab a hold of her ankles and continue to drag her through the woods. At that moment Trina just hoped and prayed that Dez was alright, still alive, and doing better than she was. Just knowing that once they reached the house shit was going to get real ugly drove Trina crazy. Just the thought of knowing all of the sick, brutal, horrible, and inhumane things that was sure to come made her wish she could somehow take her own life before she even made it back to the house. She didn't want to give those crackers the satisfaction of hearing her scream, holler, and beg for her life. She'd rather take her own life before it came down to that, but unfortunately with her wrists cuffed behind her back there was little that Trina could do. All she could do was sit and wait to be brutally murdered.

Trina thought about pleading for her life, but quickly erased the thought from her brain. She didn't have the energy nor the breath to waste on a request that she was sure would be denied.

"Were almost home," Jake said jokingly. He was happy to finally be reaching the driveway of the house, so happy that he couldn't hide the smile that was etched across his face, so happy that he could already envision Trina screaming, crying, and begging for him to kill her already.

"I'm going to teach you just what we do to bad girls like yourself," Jake said aloud as he dragged Trina over all the gravel in the driveway all the way up to the front porch. Jake turned his back towards the porch steps and dragged Trina roughly up the steps. This was a rough bumpy ride, one that Trina wouldn't soon forget.

Ann stepped up to the front door, placed her key in the key hole and gave it a turn and like that the front door eased open.

Once the reality of what was about to go down sat in, Trina went berserk. "Nooooo!" she screamed, squirming on the floor like a fish out of water. "Please don't do this! Please!"

Ann looked down at Trina and shook her head from side to side with a sick evil looking smile on her face as she slammed the front door shut.

The sight of the door being slammed shut was the final straw that made Trina lose all hope. She cried silently as Jake dragged her further inside the house.

"Don't cry now bitch!" Jake barked as he reached down and began roughly stripping Trina of her clothes. Trina did her best to stop the big white man from stripping her of her clothes by moving and squirming all over the floor. All of Trina's moving and squirming came to an end when Jake stepped down on Trina's broken ankle causing her to let out a painful howl.

"Oh okay I see," Jake said applying more pressure down to Trina's ankle. "You want to do shit the hard way. Have it your way." Jake bent down, cocked his arm back, and punched Trina dead in her mouth. The punch was so powerful that it knocked out two of her bottom teeth in the process. Jake literally then roughly snatched and ripped the clothes straight off of Trina's back.

"Go give me something else to tie this nigger bitch hands together with," Jake called over his shoulder to Ann as he smoothly reached down into his holster and removed a sharp hatchet. With a swift swipe of the blade Jake cut the plastic tie cuffs releasing Trina's wrist.

"You move and I'll kill you," Jake threatened placing the hatchet up under Trina's throat. The blade was so sharp that it pinched Trina's skin as a little trickle of blood ran down her neck and onto her exposed breast. Seconds later Ann returned with a pair of real handcuffs. She quickly bent down and handcuffed Trina's hands in front of her this time.

Once Trina's hands were cuffed, Jake effortlessly scooped her up in the air and hung the chain links of the cuffs up against the big hook that rested on the wall. Trina grunted, moaned, and winced in pain as she hung from the wall by her wrist. Her body weight hanging freely caused the handcuffs to dig and bite down even deeper into her skin cutting up her wrist in the process.

"Hang tight hun," Ann chuckled as her and Jake exited the living room leaving Trina hanging idly by her wrist. They knew for a fact that she wouldn't be going anywhere. She had no choice but to hang tight. Trina cried so much that she was surprised that she even had any tears left. Her naked body hung and swayed softly through the air. Trina thought about trying to free herself from the hook on the wall, but decided against it because the more she moved the more the metal from the handcuffs bit down and cut into her wrist.

"Fuck!" Trina shouted in frustration. She so badly wanted to hop down off the wall and kill Jake and Ann with her bare hands, watch them scream, watch them beg for their lives, and watch them hang from a fucking hook on the wall. The more Trina thought about her abductors, the more serious she became and the more determined she was to somehow break free and somehow escape from all of this madness.

"Think, think, think," Trina said in a voice barely above a whisper. Her eyes looked around searching for anything that she may be able to use to somehow break free and escape. Trina's eyes began to get misty once her eyes landed on Little Dezzy who sat strapped down to a chair in the corner. His body was burnt to a crisp. His body was so badly burnt the he was no longer recognizable and would only be able to be identified by his teeth. The longer Trina looked over at her little brother, the more she realized that there was no way she was going out like Little Dezzy and definitely not like her mother Pam. As Trina hung from the hook in the middle of the wall she could hear Jake and Ann moving around setting things up. She figured they were getting all of their tools and torture supplies ready and preparing to put some major work in on her.

"Fuck that," Trina growled as she began to start to swing her body in an attempt to free herself from the hook that rested in the middle of the wall. Each time her body swung the more the handcuffs cut and pierced through the skin on her wrist. Trina did her best to fight off the pain for as long as she could knowing that it was either this or sit around and wait to die. Sitting around waiting to die or be killed wasn't a part of the plan. After a few minutes of swinging back and forth Trina could no longer take the pain of the cuffs digging and cutting through her wrist like a razor blade.

Trina cried loudly as she continued to hang freely by her wrist. There was only one thing left for Trina to try, but the thought of it made Trina's stomach hurt. Just the thought of it alone was enough to drive any human being crazy. Trina looked around the living room one last time looking for an easier or less painful way out. Her mind and her conscience was trying to do everything to talk her out of what she was thinking about doing, but from the way it was looking Trina didn't have too many options. Not to mention the clock was working against her and at any moment Jake and Ann could walk in the living room and end her life.

"Fuck!" Trina cursed trying to mentally prepare herself for what she was getting ready to do. She took deep breaths as if she was about to give birth to a nine pound baby. Her stomach was rising and falling with each breath she took. As beads of sweat began to cover her entire face and forehead, Trina said a silent prayer asking God to watch over her and help her through the pain that was sure to come. Once Trina finished her prayer, she

122

grabbed her right thumb with her left hand and bent it back with great force until she heard a snapping and popping sound.

"CRACK!"

"Fuck!" Trina screamed at the top of her lungs as she continued to bend her thumb back until she was sure that it was broken. "Oh my God!" Trina cried when she looked up at her finger and noticed that her thumb sat in an awkward position looking like it was deformed and didn't belong on her hand. That pain seemed to help multiply the pain in her wrist as blood began to run down her arm. Trina bit down as she began trying to squeeze her right hand through the loop of the cuffs. Her thumb being broken helped the situation, but not much. She winced and cried as she used all of her might and tried to squeeze her hand through the small loop. The tight handcuffs squeezed, hurt, and assaulted Trina's already broken thumb. It made her feel as if she was dying, made her feel like jumping off of a roof would have been a better idea, a better and quicker way to go. What she was going through now was torture. With her hand halfway through the handcuffs loop Trina kept on pulling and squeezing her hand through the cuff. She could feel her broken bone moving and shifting around as she fought through the pain as best as she could as she fought and struggled to break free and escape from the cuffs. At any moment Trina felt as if she would pass out or blackout due to all the pain that her body was enduring and withstanding. She was definitely a soldier and didn't plan on stopping or giving up as long as she still had breath in her body. After a long painful fight and struggle Trina was finally able to free her hand from the cuffs loop. Her hand slid out of the cuff as her body slipped off of the hook that rested in the middle of the wall and she violently came crashing noisily down to the wood floor. Trina tried to land on her feet, but when her broken ankle made contact with the hard wood floor she instantly crumbled down to the floor. She raised her knee up to her chest and clutched her ankle squirming around on the floor in agony. Pain rested on her face as tears filled her eyes.

Now wasn't the time to worry, focus, or think about all the pain. Trina struggled back up to her feet with determination in her eyes and a focused look on her face. She stood firm on one leg as blood dripped from her chest, silver handcuffs hung from one of her wrist, and her broken thumb looked as if it didn't even belong on her hand. Trina smelled like shit and felt even worse. She hopped and hobbled on her good foot. She struggled and fought through all the pain until she finally reached the front door. With her one good hand Trina fumbled around with the locks until she was able to get the door open. The sight of daylight was like a breath of fresh air. Trina wanted to crack a smile, but knew this was far from over and she still had a long and rough road ahead of her. She hopped out the front door looking back over her shoulder repeatedly as if somebody was hot on her heels.

Trina hobbled over to Tom's tow truck and opened the door. She winced and groaned as she hopped up in the front seat. Once inside the truck Trina frantically looked in the cup holder, glove compartment, and above the sun visor for a spare set of keys to the truck.

"Shit!" Trina cursed coming up empty. Not having time to waste Trina hobbled out of the tow truck as fast as she could. With limited options the only way Trina would be able to get away from the house was to run or in her case hop.

"Body don't fail me now," Trina said to herself as she began to hop as fast as she could down the dirt road. Her body hurt and ached and felt like it would break down on her at any given moment. She moved off of pure will power and refused to be denied. It was either push her body to the limit or die and dying wasn't part of the plan. Trina wanted to die in a hospital bed and or in her sleep from old age like normal people did, not in the woods by the hands of white men who hated people just because they didn't have the same color skin. Trina's body would have to give out on her; that was the only way she was going to stop or give up. Whenever her body felt like she wanted to slow down Trina visualized Little Dezzy's body burnt to a crisp and Pam's

head detached from her body. The images in her mind helped her and gave her the motivation to keep moving and never look back.

Trina hopped as fast as she could on her one good leg. She looked up ahead and all she saw was road. She didn't have a clue how far she would have to hop until she finally reached a gas station, restaurant, or landmark for that matter. Trina figured it would be miles before she reached an establishment where she would be able to use the phone and call 911. From the looks of things she wouldn't even make it one mile with only one good leg not to mention she was beginning to feel lightheaded and dehydrated. She badly needed some water. Her mouth was so dry that her tongue felt like sandpaper. Trina would be happy with just a sip of water. That's how thirsty she was. She wasn't sure if she could make it one mile on one leg, let alone a few miles but she was more than willing to try.

PAIN

Jake placed several killing utensils on a pushcart while whistling tunelessly. He was about to have a whole lot of fun with the little black bitch that he'd been chasing and hunting for the past couple of days and now finally it was time to play and do the things that he liked to do. Jake slipped his fingers inside a pair of white latex rubber gloves with an evil smile on his face. He then turned and handed Ann a pair of gloves. Ann quickly slipped the gloves on her hands and pushed the cart out into the living room.

"We have a surprise for you." Ann's sentence got caught in her throat when she looked up and saw that Trina was no longer up on the wall. She looked down as her eyes followed a blood trail to the front door.

"Impossible," Jake blurted out as him and Ann quickly ran to the front door and snatched it open. Jake's eyes scanned left and right until he finally spotted Trina hopping on one leg down the dirt road butt naked. "There she is!" he announced as him and Ann took off down the road after Trina. The fact that Trina figured out a way to get down off the hook and escape only pissed Jake off even more and intensified his anger. The pain he planned on inflicting on Trina had now multiplied by about four. The hurt she was going to feel had just reached a whole new level. If Trina thought that she was in pain now, she was about to be in for a rude awakening.

***

Trina panted hard as she willed her leg not to give up on her. Her legs trembled like leaves in the wind and threatened to give out at any moment. Trina's fear was greater than anything she had ever felt. Her back was against the wall. The sun beaming down on her dehydrated her and took all of the fight out of her. Right now she was moving on pure heart. She was determined to make it to the finish line, determined to live and see another day, determined to not be another victim in Tom's sick and twisted game. Trina felt like she had hopped a marathon. Her eyes were wide and alert when she heard the sound of several footsteps coming up from her rear. Trina glanced over her shoulder and saw an angry faced Jake and Ann sprinting full speed ahead quickly closing the distance between them.

"Fuck, fuck, fuck!" Trina cursed as panic filled her entire body and made her began to hop even faster. Her other ankle was hurting so bad that she refused to even let it touch the ground. The sound of dirt and gravel crunching behind her grew louder and louder. Trina knew she couldn't out run anybody on just one good leg, but her pride wouldn't let her quit or stop running. If she was going to get captured she was going to get captured with her head held high looking up at her enemies and not looking down at the ground like a coward.

Trina hopped and hopped and hopped until she was tackled and roughly thrown down to the ground like a rag doll. Trina landed hard down on the graveled road and slid a few feet. The ground and gravel ripped and tore away skin from her side and shoulder.

Being that Trina only had one good leg to stand on she didn't make it too far from the house. She cried, yelled, and screamed all the way back to the house while being dragged on her back by her ankles. As Trina's back rode across the sharp and rough gravel she could only imagine what Jake and Ann planned on doing to her now once they stepped back inside the house.

Trina said a silent prayer as Ann opened the front door. She prayed that God would make all of this pain go away. If she was going to die she just asked God to make it a quick death, but for some strange reason Trina knew what was about to happen was going to be anything but quick.

The first thing Trina saw after being dragged inside the house was a pushcart filled with all types of killing instruments. "Please God no," she said out loud. Just seeing all the knives and tools made Trina's stomach turn and flip. The chances of her surviving what was to come seemed slim to none.

"So," Jake said. "You're a runner?" He nodded his head up and down. "I know just how to handle runners." Jake grabbed a hammer from off of the cart along with a long thick pointy nail. "Stand this piece of scum up!" his voice barked.

Ann quickly squatted down, grunted, and lifted Trina up to her feet. She ignored Trina's cries. In her eyes the little black girl should be glad that she was still alive and allowed to breathe the white man's air.

"Don't cry now," Ann taunted.

As Ann held Trina up, Jake firmly grabbed Trina's wrist and placed it against the wall. "Hold her wrist right there," he told Ann. Jake then placed the nail in the palm of Trina's hand.

"Please," Trina sobbed with her eyes wide with fear. Her eyes darted from Jake to Ann repeatedly. "You don't have to do this." Her pleas went on deaf ears. Trina knew that the evil white people that stood before her weren't going to let her off the hook that easy. "I'm only a kid," Trina said trying to play the age card. "Let me go and I promise you'll never hear from me again," she continued to beg. At the moment trying to talk her way out of the situation seemed like the best thing for her to do because it was the only thing she could do. "Please don't do this. I promise..."

Jake violently banged the nail through the palm of Trina's hand with the hammer stapling it to the wall.

"Arrrghh!" Trina erupted. The pain traveled from her hand all the way down to her toes. Blood dripped from around the nail that rested in the palm of her hand.

"Bet you won't be running anywhere no time soon," Jake said chuckling. Then he quickly moved on to the other hand. Ann held Trina's other hand out while Jake positioned the nail in the center of her palm and with a hard swing with the hammer he watched as the nail punctured her hand, turning her hand into a bloody mess.

128

Jake and Ann took a step back and laughed as they watched Trina hang from the wall looking like she had been crucified. The more pain Trina was in, the more Jake and Ann seemed to be enjoying themselves and they most definitely enjoyed the view of the little black girl being nailed up to the wall.

"You think we should do her feet too?" Ann asked with a raised brow. Trina being nailed to the wall wasn't good enough for her. It didn't satisfy her, didn't appease her, and didn't float her boat. Ann needed more. She wouldn't be happy until more pain was inflicted.

"Yeah, we can do her feet," Jake replied with a smile. "Let's get her cleaned up first." He grabbed a bottle of rubbing alcohol, twisted off the cap, and then tossed the cap down to the floor. "Do me a favor," Jake said glancing over at Ann. "Go put a big pot of water on the stove," he said with a devilish grin. "We about to sterilize this bitch."

Ann smiled, and then went off into the kitchen to do as she was told. Just the thought of sterilizing Trina cause a smile to spread across her face; a smile that wouldn't be coming off of Ann's face while they had Trina in their possession. Ann disappeared into the kitchen and the sound of pots and pans rattling and banging could be heard.

"I'mma show you just what we do to runners," Jake said smirking as he splashed some of the alcohol all over Trina's body and open wounds. He laughed at the sight of her grunting and gritting her teeth in pain.

"You thought trying to sneak out of here was a smart idea?" Jake asked and then poured some of alcohol over both of Trina's palms.

Trina screamed out in pain as the alcohol sunk deep into the core of the open wounds. The alcohol stung and burned. It made Trina feel like her entire body was on fire, like she was being bitten by a million mosquitoes, like she had acid flowing through her veins.

"Kill me already!" Trina yelled.

"You wouldn't be so lucky," Jake said continuing to splash rubbing alcohol all over Trina's battered and bruised body. "But I promise you going to wish that I had killed you."

WE ARE A TEAM

"I don't know how much longer I can walk," Frankie said with an exhausted look on her face. Her legs were beginning to feel like noodles, like they were made out of rubber bands, and like she was walking on glass legs that was sure to break any second.

"Hang in there," Dez told her. There had to be a way out of the cave somewhere around here. If there was a way in, then it had to be a way out. All Dez had to do was make his way through the maze and find an exit. Dying in a cave wasn't a part of his plan. This wasn't how he wanted his legacy to end. This wasn't how he wanted to be remembered. When Dez died he wanted to die with honor and not in a dirty rat infested cave somewhere.

Dez tried his hardest not to think about Trina. He could only imagine what she was going through right now and that only made him want to find a way out of the cave even more so he could be there to protect her. In his eyes she was still his little girl. Dez might not have been there in Trina's past, but he was damn sure going to be there for her when she needed him the most and that was now.

Dez draped Frankie's arm around his neck and helped her keep moving. They had come too far to stop now. Frankie was tired and wanted to give up, but her heart wouldn't let her. Her heart wouldn't allow her to be a quitter. Her heart was forcing her to keep moving, forcing her to give it her all, forcing her to use every ounce of strength she had in her body.

"I'm okay," Frankie said weakly. She forced a weak smile trying to show Dez that she was okay. Her arm was bleeding badly and her body was badly injured. She was starving and on top of all that, she felt like she was dying of thirst.

Dez knew that Frankie was trying to convince herself more than him that she was okay, but Dez could see right through her front. He too was tired and badly injured, so if he was feeling it he knew Frankie definitely had to be feeling it. Up ahead Dez saw a ray of light. It looked like the sun was casting through some kind of a hole. Dez didn't want to get his hopes up, but from the way it was looking he may have found a way out. The further Dez and Frankie walked, the brighter and bigger the ray of light became.

"Is that a way out?" Frankie asked in a dry raspy voice looking up ahead. The ray of light looked to be shining through a small hole in the wall.

"Wait here," Dez said helping Frankie take a seat on the ground. He then walked over to the hole in the wall to further investigate and see just where the ray of light was coming from. Upon further investigation, Dez saw that the wall was made of hard cold dirt. He could tell that the dirt, water, and cold air had turned the mud into a hard layer of what felt like concrete. Dez removed the kitchen knife from his back pocket and began to chip away at the small hole that rested in the wall. *"Come on,"* he grunted as he worked his arm trying to make the hole big enough for him to squeeze through. The muscles in his arm burned like crazy like he had been doing pull-ups for the past hour. It hurt so bad to the point where he had to switch arms and continue to chip away with the other hand. The more Dez worked the knife, the bigger the small hole in the wall became. Dez continued to chip away at the wall for thirty minutes straight alternating hands until the hole was big enough for him to squeeze through.

"Come on!" Dez called out to Frankie as he slipped the kitchen knife back down in his back pocket. He locked his fingers together turning his hands into a handmade cup. Frankie planted her dirty barefoot in his hands as he boosted her up in the air. Frankie outstretched her arms grabbed the top of the man sized hole and struggled as she did her best to use every ounce of strength inside of her body to pull herself up out the hole. Frankie's arms violently shook and trembled. Then they gave out on her and she came crashing down into Dez's arms.

"I can't," Frankie said in a, *I give up* tone of voice. Her body language said that she had made it as far as she could go. A defeated look sat on her face. Frankie turned and glanced at Dez giving him a look that said she was sorry, but she couldn't continue any further.

"I can't let you go out like that," Dez said shaking his head. "Not like this." He jumped up and grabbed the top of the manhole. He too struggled to lift himself out of the hole. With half of his body above ground and other half underground, Dez pulled himself out of the manhole. To anybody else at first sight it would have looked like he was climbing out of a grave. Dez deeply inhaled the fresh air as if his head had been held underwater for over two minutes. "Thank you Jesus!" he said breathing heavily while looking up at the sky.

"Go on without me!" Dez heard Frankie scream from down below in the cave.

Dez ignored Frankie's request. He rolled over on his stomach and outstretched his arm reaching down into the cave. "Grab my hand."

"No," Frankie replied. "Go on without me. All I'mma do is slow you down. Go and find your daughter. She needs you more than I do." She paused for a second. "I'll be fine; I promise. Just don't forget to send some help for me." She flashed a weak stained toothy smile.

"I'm not leaving without you!" Dez barked. "Now jump up here and grabbed my hand!" he demanded.

"I can't!"

"Yes you can!"

"Just go on without me Dez!"

"Ain't no quitters over here!" Dez barked. "Now get your ass up! Jump up here and grab my fucking hand!" His voice was sharp and stern and it was igniting a reaction out of Frankie.

Frankie slowly rose to her feet, looked up at Dez's hand, took a deep breath, and on a silent count of three she jumped up and tried to grab Dez's hand, but failed miserably. Frankie attempted to jump up and grab Dez's hand three more times only to get the same results.

"I can't!" she screamed out in frustration as tears streamed down her cheeks.

"I'm not leaving here without you," Dez told her. It was no way he could just turn his back and leave Frankie for dead in the middle of nowhere down in a cave. He wasn't a flat leaver and would never be able to forgive himself if he left Frankie down in the cave to die. "Come on try again!" he demanded. Frankie stood a while, squatted down, and then leaped up as high as she could. Dez reached down as him and Frankie's hands connected wrist to wrist.

"I got you!" he grunted.

Dez struggled using all of his strength and all of the muscles in his back to pull Frankie up out of the cave. Frankie may have looked slim, but pulling her up out of the cave with one hand made it feel as if she weighed over two hundred pounds.

"Don't drop me," Frankie gasped looking up at Dez.

Once Dez got Frankie up to the top of the cave she quickly used her other hand to help pull herself above ground.

Frankie and Dez lay flat on their backs staring up at the pretty blue sky as they sucked in as much air as possible.

"We made it," Frankie smiled with her eyes closed. She had been stuck down in the dirty rat infested cave for days and was happy to finally be out of the dark, stinky cave.

"Thank you Jesus!"

"Thank you Jesus is right!" Dez said and then sat straight up and looked around taking in his surroundings. He looked right then left and spotted the house where it all began; Tom's house. He aggressively tapped Frankie on her shoulder. "Look!"

"What?" Frankie said sitting up and staring at the house. She too had lost her entire family in Tom's house. She silently stared at it for second. She stared at it as if the boogie man resided inside, as if staring at it long enough would bring back her family.

"You think your daughter is in there?"

"It's only one way to find out."

GUESS WHO

D ez and Frankie cautiously made their way over to the house. Something in Dez's gut told him that Trina was in the house more than likely begging and fighting for her life. As bad as Dez didn't want Trina to be inside of the house, he had a feeling that she was. The closer he and Frankie made it to the house, the louder the sound of screams could be heard. Once Dez heard the screams, he immediately knew that the voice behind the screams belonged to Trina.

"She's in there," Dez whispered to Frankie as they stepped up to the front porch. Dez tiptoed up the wooden porch being sure not to alert whoever was inside the house of him and Frankie's arrival. Dez inched his way over and peeked inside the window. What he saw inside the window made his stomach turn. He felt vomit come up and hit the back of his throat. He made a gurgling sound as he threw up what remaining food he still had down his stomach.

"You alright?" Frankie whispered as she joined Dez's side and peeked inside the front window. Immediately her eyes locked on a young teenage black girl who looked to be crucified to the wall. "Oh my God!" Her hand shot up to her mouth in shock.

When Dez was done throwing up, he walked up to the front door grabbed the handle and twisted the knob and was shocked to find out that the front door was left open. He entered the house and his eyes widened with rage when he saw a big white man shoving the handle of a dirty oily wrench forcefully in and out of Trina's vagina. The sick perverted look on the white man's face only made Dez even more furious. Dez looked over and saw Ann standing over on the sideline holding a long leather whip in her hand with a sick smile on her face.

Before Dez realized what was going on he had already taken off running full speed growling loudly heading straight for the big white man.

Jake looked up and saw an angry looking black man charging him with incredible speed. Before he got a chance to react Dez hit him with great force sending both of them crashing and tumbling over the push cart full of knives and tools designed to inflict pain on a person. The cart flipped over making a loud rattling and clinking noise as all the tools fell scattering all over the floor. Dez landed on top of Jake and began raining hard punches down on his face trying to break his face, trying to rearrange Jake's once handsome features, and trying to break something with each punch.

As Dez stood over Jake pounding his face, out of nowhere he heard a loud snapping noise, then felt a sharp stinging and burning pain on his back. He looked back over his shoulder and saw Ann standing behind him with a leather whip in her hand. She quickly swung the whip and watched as the whip snapped and bit like a cobra cutting through Dez's shirt and removing a nice chunk of skin from his back in the process.

Ann went to swing the whip for a third time, but stumbled sideways as Frankie caught her with a quick rabbit punch to her jaw. Frankie quickly followed up with of vicious left, right combination to the face not giving Ann a chance to regain her balance. Ann fought, struggled, and did her best to keep her footing by backpedaling as the fight spilled off into the kitchen.

Trina hung nailed from the wall watching the brawl and rumble play out right before her eyes. When she saw Dez and some strange woman that she had never seen before come busting into the house out the corner of her eye she thought she was dreaming until the blows started flying. Trina wanted to jump in and join the brawl but with her hands being nailed to the wall all she could do at the moment was cheer Dez and the mysterious woman on and hope and pray that when it was all said and done Dez came out on top.

"That's right!" Trina shouted from up above. "Tear their asses up!"

Jake had somehow made it up to his feet trying to fight back, but couldn't seem to focus on his attacker with his head violently snapping from left to right from hard stiff punches delivered by Dez. Dez's hands were lightning quick, but also packed a nice amount of power.

Jake felt his left eye close shut and knew he would have to change something in his strategy before he got humiliated by getting knocked out by a black guy. Jake faked like he was about to throw a punch and went low. He grabbed Dez's legs and scooped him up and ran full speed into a wall violently ramming Dez's back into the wall. A loud booming noise erupted when Dez's back hit the wall, followed by a loud grunt. Jake bent down and slammed Dez down through the wooden coffee table. Once Dez's back hit the floor he felt Jake's large hands wrapped around his neck. Jake squeezed hard with his hands turning into vise grips. He wanted to squeeze the life out of Dez, so later on he could brag and boast to his friends about how he had killed a nigger with his bare hands. He wanted to get this chapter of the book over and done with and move on and finish what he has started with Trina who still hung freely from the wall with a scared and shocked look on her face.

Dez clawed at Jake's large hands trying to loosen the tight grip that he had around his neck, but his efforts had little to no effect on the big man. Dez's hand blindly searched the floor until his hand made contact with a scalpel that had fell from off the push cart. Dez gripped the scalpel and jammed it in Jake's eye and then gave the scalpel a hard twist. Immediately blood came gushing out of Jake's eye directly down onto Dez's face.

Jake howled out in pain as he released his grip from around Dez's neck and grabbed his eye hoping to stop the bleeding. Dez quickly shot up to his feet, removed the kitchen knife from his back pocket, and went to work on Jake. Blood covered Dez's wrist as he sliced, cut, and stabbed Jake repeatedly until the big white man finally collapsed down to the hard wood floor.

"That's right!" Trina cheered Dez on. The sight of Jake getting what he deserved brought a smile to her face. Trina wasn't a violent person nor did she like to see people get hurt, but watching Dez kill Jake made her feel good inside, made her feel mighty, made her feel happy to be on the winning team. "Cut his fucking head off, like they did Mommy!" she shouted.

Dez stood over Jake's wounded body looking down in the man's eyes. He saw no fear, no regret, and no remorse. The eyes of a tortured soul stared back at him.

"What kind of people would do this to another human being?" Dez asked looking down at Jake. "What did we ever do to you to deserve this?"

"You niggers should never step foot in the white man's part of town," Jake growled staring up at Dez. "You niggers just don't get it," he chuckled. "But don't worry Tom is going to teach you niggers."

"So, this is how you teach us?" Dez nodded toward his daughter hanging freely by her hands from the wall. "By killing and torturing kids?"

"Fuck you and fuck that little nigger bitch hanging from the wall over there!" Jake flashed a bloody smile. "When Tom catches wind of this, he's going to finish off the job that I started with that wrench over there," Jake said and then broke out into a laughing fit. He laughed like he had just told the funniest joke in the world. Right in the middle of his laugh Dez bent down and plunged the kitchen knife in and out of Jake's throat and then Dez jammed the knife down in Jake's heart killing him instantly.

Dez continued to stab Jake well after he was dead. If he could, Dez would have killed the white man that lie before him a hundred more times and not lose a night of sleep.

"That's enough. He's already dead!" Trina yelled from the wall snapping Dez out of his trance.

Dez removed the bloody knife from Jake's body, slid it down in his pocket, and then walked over to the wall and looked and tried to figure out how he was going to get Trina down from off the wall as painless as possible. Dez examined Trina's hands closely and saw the two nails were pinned all the way down at her bloody palms. "Damn," he whispered as he searched the floor until he found a hammer lying over in the corner.

"This might hurt a little bit, but I have to do it," he told Trina as he slowly walked back over to where she hung with the hammer hanging loosely by his side.

"Do what you got to do. Just make it quick," Trina said shutting her eyes anticipating the pain that she knew was sure to come. Just the sight of the hammer in Dez's hand made Trina's whole body tingle as the hairs on the back of her neck stood at attention.

Dez grabbed Trina's wrist with one hand and used the back part of the hammer to remove the nail from the palm of her hand. Blood, skin and meat spilled from Trina's palm as Dez removed and eased the nail out of her hand.

Trina let out a loud eardrum ringing shriek as she kept her eyes shut tight. The sight of the nail being removed from the palm of her hand would've been too much for her eyes at the moment. Pain flooded her entire body causing her body to shake uncontrollably. The sound of the nail hitting the floor was music to Trina's ears. One down and one left to go.

***

Meanwhile, in the kitchen Frankie and Ann fought for their lives breaking any and everything in their path. Scratching, biting, hair pulling, and eye gouging took place. It was a loud, noisy, a nasty fight. It was like a street fight, no rules and no one to step in between the two women and break up the fight. The refrigerator, stove, counter, and walls made it feel like the two women were fighting in a phone booth instead of a kitchen.

Frankie grabbed Ann's hair with two hands and dragged her around and throughout the kitchen while talking shit to her the entire time.

"Bitch you done fucked with the wrong one," Frankie growled as she proceeded to beat Ann like she had stolen something.

Frankie's power hand had swollen up on her, but a little bit of swelling wasn't going to stop her from getting in Ann's ass. Ann tried to scurry away from the physical abuse, but with Frankie having a grip on her hair she didn't get far.

"Don't try to run now bitch!" Frankie landed of vicious uppercut, then followed up with another one, then another one, and then another one. Frankie went to swing Ann down to the floor by her hair, but in the process Ann grabbed a rolling pin from off the counter, closed her eyes, and swung the rolling pin blindly. It just so happened to connect right on the bridge of Frankie's nose breaking it instantly.

Frankie grabbed her nose with two hands as blood spilled from between her fingers. While Frankie was stunned, Ann used this opportunity to her advantage. She picked up the pot of boiling water from off the stove with extreme quickness. She turned and tried to splash the boiling water if Frankie's face trying to blind and scar her for life. Every time Frankie looked in the mirror Ann wanted her to always remember her.

"Shit!" Frankie cursed as she ducked down and dropped to the floor just as Ann tried to assault her with the boiling water. The boiling water caught Frankie on the back of her neck as well as part of her back. Frankie dropped to the floor withering in agony, holding the back of her neck. Seeing that she didn't catch Frankie the way she wanted to with the boiling water, Ann quickly snatched the rolling pin from the counter and hit Frankie across the back of her head knocking Frankie unconscious. Ann quickly jumped down onto Frankie's back and proceeded to bash the black woman's skull in with the rolling pin. Ann's growls got louder and louder each time the rolling pin came in contact with Frankie's skull.

Ann grabbed the rolling pin with two hands and raised it high above her head with murderous intentions clouding her brain and fire dancing her eyes. She wanted to kill Frankie so bad that her hands began to tremble and shake.

Just as Ann got ready to bring the rolling pin down one last time on Frankie's head, her head violently jerk to the side as she fell in what looked like slow motion face first down onto the kitchen floor. Behind Ann stood Dez and in his hand he held a bloody hammer and a mean look on his face.

Trina hobbled in the kitchen, looked down, and saw Ann laid out face first on the kitchen floor with blood leaking from the side of her head. Trina used her wounded hands and grabbed the dish rack filled with dishes and tossed them down on the top of Ann's head. The sound of plates breaking and pots and pans rattling erupted throughout the kitchen. Trina then quickly hobbled over towards the sink, turned the cold water on, ducked her head under the faucet, and began to slurp and drink as much water as she could. The cold faucet water tasted like pure spring water to Trina. She guzzled as much as she could and then released a loud drawn out burp.

Once Trina was done, Dez dipped his head under the faucet and enjoyed a nice cool drink of water. He cut the water off, looked down, and saw Trina searching through Ann's pockets.

Trina looked up and said, "No car keys." She stood to her feet, looked down at Ann's unconscious body and spit on her. "I hate you!" Her words came straight from the heart. She hated Tom, Ann, and anyone else who had anything to do with hurting and killing innocent people. In Trina's mind, Ann and anyone else like her deserved to die, a horrible painful death, a death that would be remembered for a lifetime.

"I'm gonna chop this bitch's head off just like she did mommy," Trina said searching the kitchen floor for something sharp enough to detach Ann's head from her body. It was time to even the score and let Ann see what it felt like when the rabbit had the gun.

"We don't have time for that," Dez told Trina.

"No, fuck that!" Trina spat. "She chopped my mother's head off, so now I'm going to chop this bitch head off!"

"I know your mother didn't raise you like that. I know she didn't," Dez said in a calm soft voice. "If Pam was still alive she wouldn't want you to do this. It's over. We free to go. Let's go home!"

"No! They killed mommy and Little Dezzy and now they have to pay!" Trina reached down and picked up a sharp pointy steak knife.

Before Trina got a chance to do anything Dez walked up on her and gently grabbed her wrist. "Put the knife down baby," he said softly looking down into his daughter's eyes. He knew Trina was upset and had every right to feel the way she did, but if he was to allow her to follow through with her actions, those same actions would be sure to haunt her for the rest of her life and Dez couldn't allow that to happen. "Let's go home," he repeated in a soft tone.

Trina let go of the steak knife, buried her head in Dez's chest, and sobbed quietly. "I miss my mommy…"

"I know you do baby," Dez said as he gently rubbed Trina's back trying to comfort and soothe her. "I miss mommy to," he assured her. "Let's go home. This nightmare is over." Dez began to lead Trina out of the kitchen until Trina stopped suddenly.

"What about her?" Trina nodded at Frankie who laid sprawled across the floor in a puddle of her own blood. "You think she's dead?"

"I don't know," Dez shrugged. He didn't want to think the worse, but from where he was standing Frankie looked to be as dead as a door knob. He didn't see her chest or stomach moving up and down and that alone told him that she wasn't breathing.

"We can't just leave her here like that," Trina said looking up at Dez. It wouldn't feel right in her heart to just leave Frankie dead on the kitchen floor. After all she had risked her own life to help save Trina's life.

"We'll send help back here as soon as possible for her," Dez said. "With our injuries we wouldn't make it but so far with her anyway." He nodded down towards Trina's broken ankle.

"Okay, well at least check and see if she's got a pulse before we just leave her for dead," Trina said with major concern in her voice. She didn't know Frankie personally, but still didn't feel that it was right to just leave her like that. It was bad enough that she couldn't save Pam and Little Dezzy, the least she could do was try and save another innocent victim.

Dez headed over towards where Frankie lay, and then stopped dead in his tracks when he heard the front door open and then slam shut with great force. Immediately his heart leapt up into his throat out of fear. Dez had been through enough ever since he arrived on Tom's property and was ready for the nightmare to finally be over and done with. Dez and Trina both made their way from the kitchen back into the living room only to find Tom standing in the middle of the room with a sick, scary, no nonsense look on his face. His face was covered in blood. He stood shirtless, and weighing in at two-thirty ready to do somebody dirty. In his hand he held a sharp hatchet. Tom held the handle of the hatchet so tight that Dez could see the veins popping out of his muscular arms. Tom's eyes were fixed on Dez. This was the first black man to ever give him this many problems, the first black man to ever make him work so hard, the first black man to ever push him to the limit, and give him a run for his money.

Dez removed the kitchen knife from his back pocket and turned and faced Trina. "Get up out of here baby!"

"What about you?" Trina asked with a worried look on her face. "I'm not leaving you!"

"Go on without me. I promise I'll catch up with you." Dez flashed his famous smile. "Go find us some help."

Trina looked at Tom and then back at Dez. "You sure you will be alright?"

"Positive," Dez replied and bent down and kissed Trina on the cheek.

Trina gave Dez a fist bump and then hobbled past Tom towards the front door. Trina reached the front door, stopped, turned back, and glanced at Dez. Her body language was full of confidence and showed a lot of bravery, but her eyes told an entirely different story. Her eyes told Dez that she was afraid and scared and didn't know how this whole situation was going to play out. Her eyes also told Dez that she didn't want to leave his side or be away from him again.

"I love you baby!" Dez called out.

"I love you too daddy," Trina replied with a smile on her face. In these past couple of days Dez had not only earned her respect, but he had also earned Trina's love. For a man to go through everything he went through to try and keep Trina alive, it had to be love.

The bright smile that was plastered on Dez's face was priceless and if Trina could keep this memory for the rest of her life she would, but right now she had to get going. She looked Dez in his eyes and said "Kill that motherfucker!"

Dez nodded his head and like that Trina disappeared out the front door and was gone.

Dez and Tom stared each other down for a couple more seconds. In all reality the stare down lasted for maybe ten seconds, but it felt and seemed like an eternity.

Once the quick stare down was over, Tom made his way towards Dez. With murderous intension in his eyes and a sharp weapon in his hand, Tom planned on settling this score once and for all. Immediately Dez got into a defensive stance preparing to do battle until either him or his opponent was no longer breathing.

Tom took off in a full sprint growling and charging like a pit-bull. Before Dez got a chance to react Tom had taken a swipe at his wrist with the hatchet. The sharp blade made contact with Dez's forearm causing him to drop the kitchen knife that he held down to the floor. Immediately Dez grabbed a hold of Tom and the two struggled. With Tom's muddy boots slipping, Dez's sneakers squeaking, they fought for the sharp weapon in Tom's hand. The weapon in Tom's hand had a blade on it that could cut through bones. They slammed each other up against the wall, tussled, and crashed into the entertainment system and then the table.

Tom forcefully drove Dez back into the wall and planted his forearm up under Dez's throat trying to cut off his air supply. While getting choked Dez still held a firm grip on the wrist that Tom held the hatchet in. Dez tried to sweep Tom's legs up from under him, but the position he was in stopped his attempt. They battled across the junk filled floor and wrestled eye to eye. Dez landed a knee to Tom's groin causing him to double over in pain. Dez gritted his teeth, grunted, and shoved the blade toward Tom's chest. The look on Tom's face changed from anger to desperation and fear. Tom and Dez struggled, strength against strength, in an arm wrestle that lasted for what seemed like forever. This was a battle that both men refused to lose. The sharp blade inching closer and closer towards Tom's chest caused sweat to run down his face. With limited options Tom landed a head butt to the bridge of Dez's nose. The loud cracking sound and the instant flow of blood announced that his nose was broken.

Tom landed a quick left hook on Dez's face and then pushed Dez up off him, separating the two. Now Tom had room to work with. He held the hatchet in a firm grip, stood in a low hunch, and inched his way towards Dez. Giving up was never a thought in his mind.

"Shit," Dez growled, as his eyes watered from being hit in the nose, with the tears slightly affecting his vision. Dez looked down and saw the kitchen knife a few feet away on the floor. He knew he wouldn't be able to make it to the knife without being carved up into little pieces by the sharp hatchet. Dez wiped his eyes, then quickly removed his belt from around his waist, wrapped it tightly once around his hand, and let the buckle swing freely turning the belt into a deadly weapon. Dez then began swinging the belt like it was a pair of nun-chucks. Dez struck Tom on the side of his face with the belt like the bite of a cobra causing Tom's DNA to spill in red.

Tom took a step back and eyed the belt that hung from Dez's hand. His eye stung and burned badly. Tom hadn't expected the black man to be this much trouble, but it was far too late to turn back now. A fight to the death was taking place and Tom's mind was already made up. He wasn't going to lose. Just as Tom got ready to make his move, he saw Ann stagger up out of the kitchen into the living room. Blood leaked from her head as she used the wall to help hold herself up.

Tom dug down in his pocket, removed a key chain that had a single key attached to the link and tossed it to Ann. "The girl escaped up the road. Go take care of her," Tom ordered as he watched Ann stagger out the front door to take care of the task that lie ahead.

The split second decision where Tom glanced at Ann was all Dez needed. He swung the belt and watched as it struck Tom's wrist like another cobra bite. The hatchet dropped from Tom's hand and made a loud clinking noise as it hit the floor. Tom thought about reaching down for it, but decided against it when he saw Dez inching towards him with the belt buckle swinging from his hand.

Instead Tom charged Dez, grabbed him, hit him hard, lifted Dez up, and both men went airborne crashing down loudly to the floor. Both men hit the floor swinging. Tom and Dez quickly made it back up to their feet and continued to go at it. It was a violent noisy fight that moved from wall to wall and up and down the hallway. Dez snapped off a quick eight punch combination, left – right, left – right, left – left, right – right. Tom blocked and weaved as many of the incoming punches as possible, but a few slipped through his guard.

Tasting his own blood enraged Tom. Dez quickly lunged for Tom's legs trying to take him down to the floor, but Tom threw spearing elbows and knees at a relentless pace, shutting off Dez's take down attempt with an elbow to the temple. The blow stunned Dez, but didn't take him out. Tom then pulled his head down for a nose shattering knee to the face. That final blow put Dez's lights out.

Tom stood breathing heavy, staring down at Dez. It was finally over. He had finally defeated the black man. Tom raised his leg and gave Dez's face a hard stomp for good measures. Tom then quickly grabbed Dez's belt from off the floor and bound Dez's hands together at the wrist. Once that was done Tom looked down at Dez, then in a quick leg motion dropped Dez on some Hulk Hogan shit. The impact from the leg drop caused Dez's body to move, but he still remained out like a light. Tom cleared his throat and released a glob of spit down onto Dez's face.

Tom laughed out loud as he picked up Dez's ankles and dragged him all the way over to the basement door. He was about to make Dez wish he had been dead a long time ago, make him wish he had never gotten stranded, make him wish that he was never born. Tom opened the door to the basement, grabbed Dez's ankles and dragged his unconscious body down the basement steps. It was a long, loud, bumpy ride. Dez couldn't feel it now, but when he woke up he was sure to feel the bumps and bruises.

Down in the basement sat a table. Not just any ordinary table, but an operating table. This operating table had leather straps at the bottom for a person's ankles and straps at the top for the wrist.

Tom reached down and effortlessly scooped Dez up and roughly dropped him down on top of the table. He took his time and walked around the table strapping Dez's ankles and wrist down to the table. Over in the corner on a shelf sat several killing instruments, which included a chain saw, an ax, an iron, and a crow bar just to name a few. Tom stood in front of the shelf, grabbed the iron, and plugged it into the outlet. While he waited for the iron to heat up, he walked over and looked down at the dirty black nigger that lay before him and for the first time in a while, a wicked smile appeared on Tom's face.

DON'T STOP

Trina hopped and hobbled down the dirt road as fast as she could. She badly wanted to stop and take a rest. Her body was in pain and was on the verge of breaking down, but a voice in the back of her mind kept screaming, *"Don't stop! Don't stop!"* Trina knew if she did stop she was as good as dead, so stopping to take a rest wasn't an option. Trina used everything in her to keep moving. The whole time while hobbling down the road Trina's mind went back to Dez. She knew Dez and Tom were inside the house killing each other. She just hoped and prayed that Dez would come out of the situation on top. Images of Dez and Tom going at it filled Trina's brain like a motion pictured movie. The sound of a car coming from behind her at a fast pace brought her back to reality. Trina glanced back over her shoulder and saw a burgundy car moving at a fast pace leaving a big dust cloud behind.

"Aw shit!" Trina cursed and then tried to put a little pep in her step. She gave it her all, but due to her circumstances she could only move, but so fast. The more Trina hopped down the dirt road the louder the engine on the car could be heard as it closed the gap in between the two.

Trina glanced over her shoulder again and saw the burgundy car coming straight at her. With only a split second to make a decision she jumped out of the way and landed down in a ditch just as the burgundy car flew past her. A second later and she would have been road kill and would have had to get scraped up off the ground.

As Trina lay in the ditch, the sound of tires screeching could be heard as the burgundy car came to a sudden stop. Ann hopped out the driver's seat with a .22 in her right hand and an evil look on her face. Her head still hurt badly as blood leaked out of the open wound.

"Move bitch and I'll put a bullet in your head," Ann warned. She reached down and roughly pulled Trina up to her feet by her hair. She slapped her across the face with the gun trying to knock out a few of her teeth in the process. She was trying to knock some sense into the young black girl. Ann escorted Trina over to the burgundy car and then forced her into the front seat. She kept the barrel of the .22 pointed at Trina while she walked around the front of the car, then slid in the driver's seat. Ann viciously slapped Trina across the side of her head with the gun out of anger.

"I should blow your fucking had off right now," Ann growled. She held the steering wheel with one hand and shoved the .22 in the side of Trina's ribs with the other hand. "I know my husband is going to have something real nice in store for you when we get back," Ann said smiling, and then guided the burgundy car back around towards the house. Every time Trina felt that she was distancing herself from the house, she somehow got dragged back towards the house like some kind of magnetic force drew her towards the house; sort of like a moth to a flame.

"Why are you doing this?" Trina asked, while trying to form some kind of plan in her head on how she could somehow escape from the car without getting herself killed in the process. "Haven't you caused me and my family enough pain already?"

"Hmmp!" Ann huffed. "After all the shit you and that nigger father of yours done put me and my husband through, you want us to cut you some slack? You want us to be lenient on you right?" Ann chuckled. "You wouldn't be so lucky. I'm going to watch you and that piece of shit nigger father of yours die a slow and painful death."

"Why are you so evil?" Trina asked with a disgusted look on her face. She just couldn't understand how a human being could be so evil, so unhuman, so barbaric, and cruel. "What have black people ever done to you to make you want to do something like this? Why do you hate us so much?"

149

"That's where you're wrong," Ann smirked. "I don't hate just black people. I hate spics, Jews, Muslims, you name it, so please don't get it mixed and screwed. It ain't nothing special about you niggers."

"Let me go," Trina said. "Let me go and I promise I won't kill you. I promise I'll spare your life and let you live to see another day," she told her.

"You got some motherfucking nerve," Ann growled. She couldn't believe the audacity of the little black bitch; raggedy Ann in the flesh minus the clothes and colorful dreads. "You promise to spare my life?" she repeated taking her eyes off the road for a second to glance over at Trina. "Let me make you a little promise, how abo---."

"How about you shut the fuck up!" Trina barked cutting Ann off in the middle of her sentence. "I wish I had a dick right now, so I could shove it in your mouth and then maybe you would shut the fuck up!"

With the quickness of a cat Ann turned and back slapped Trina across the face with the gun. As the gun made contact with Trina's face she quickly grabbed Ann's wrist and held on to it for dear life. The gun discharged twice as Ann fought with one hand to keep the wheel straight, with the other hand she fought and struggled with Trina over possession of the fire arm.

Trina growled and grunted as she did her best to try and disarm Ann. The burgundy car swerved and jerked from side to side. Trina figured if she was going to die she might as well go out on her own terms. As the two continued to fight over the gun, Trina bit down into Ann's forearm biting out a big chunk of skin and meat. Blood covered Trina's mouth and smeared across her cheeks as she went in for another bite. The gun discharged again and two loud shots filled the car. Ann jerked her arm back and elbowed Trina in the face causing her head to violently jerk back and collide with the head rest. In the process Ann was able to jerk her arm free out of Trina's grip. The pain from the two bite wounds slowed her reflexes down a bit. Ann regained control of the gun and aimed the business end at Trina. The look in Ann's eyes told

Trina that she was about to blow her brains all over the passenger window. With limited options, Trina moved off instinct. Her hand quickly shot out and grabbed the steering wheel and jerked it hard to the right. The tires on the burgundy car squealed loudly as it jerked, turned, swerved, and then flipped over. Trina and Ann's bodies somersaulted, crashed up into the roof, and then back down, as the car flipped over at least twelve times before resting upside down on its roof. The burgundy car lay wrecked and smoking, resting idly on the side of the road.

Three minutes later Trina finally came back around. Blood trickled from a brand new gash that opened up on top of her head and blood also dripped from Trina's earlobe. At first Trina's vision was a little blurry and she couldn't remember where she was or how she had gotten there. Trina blinked repeatedly until she fully gained her vision back. She turned her head slightly to her left and as soon as she spotted Ann lying unconscious in an awkward position it all started to come back to her. All the torturing, pain, and suffering that Ann and her husband had put her through all came back to her in a flash. Trina spotted the .22 hand gun laying inches away from Ann's head. She slowly reached out, grabbed the gun, and then placed it to the side of Ann's head. A single tear escaped Trina's eye and her hand started to tremble. Her hand trembled not because she was scared to kill Ann, but because she had wanted to kill Ann so bad, because she was finally about to get payback for all the cruel and nasty shit Ann and Tom had done to so many others, because she was finally about to give retribution to Ann for what she and her husband had done to her mother and brother.

"I hate you," Trina said in a low whisper just as she pulled the trigger. Ann's head violently jerked back as blood splashed all over the place including all over Trina's face. Trina then cried tears of Joy as she army crawled out of the broken passenger's window, dragged her wounded and battered body across broken glass and shards of metal from the car, and then struggled back to her feet.

Trina had been naked for so long that she didn't even realize that she was naked anymore. She looked up and saw the house, the same house that she had tried to escape from numerous times. The same house that Dez was still trapped inside going through only God knew what. Trina removed the clip from the small gun and counted out two rounds, plus the one in the head made three bullets in total. She shoved the clip back inside the gun and hobbled on back towards the house. The only thing on Trina's mind right now was killing Tom if Dez hadn't already beaten her to the punch. Out of nowhere Trina felt as if she had just gotten a second wind from somewhere. She had a new sudden burst of energy. She wondered if the gun in her hand had anything to do with it or was it the rush from her getting her first kill.

Whatever it was, it had Trina feeling like she was on some type of drugs and it only made Trina even more determined to kill Tom. She reached the front of the house, slowly inched her way up the porch steps, and then stopped at the front door. She held the gun in a firm one handed grip, counted to three in her mind, and then burst through the front door. Her arm swept the empty living room. With only three shots remaining in the gun Trina knew she had to be smart and precise with each shot. At first sight the living room looked like a tornado had been through it twice. Trina paid the mess no mind as she inched further and further inside the house. She wanted to hold the gun with two hands, but her broken thumb prevented that from happening. Her injuries prevented her from moving at a pace that she would have preferred. After scanning the entire living room Trina moved on towards the kitchen, looking straight ahead not wanting to make eye contact with Little Dezzy's burnt up body. Trina stepped foot in the kitchen and the first thing she noticed was that Frankie's body was no longer on the kitchen floor. Before she could give what she had discovered any thought, the sound of Dez howling out in pain lead her towards a door in the middle of the hallway. A door she hadn't noticed before, that on first glance one would have missed. As Trina cautiously inched her way towards the door she could hear Dez's cries getting louder and louder. Trina reached the door and placed her ear to it trying to see if she could hear anything that might let her know exactly what was going on behind the door, so she could have a chance to fully prepare herself for the horror that she was sure to see. One more loud scream was all it took. Trina grabbed the knob, turned it, and opened it slowly. The first thing she saw was a long flight of steps and then she heard more screaming. Trina had never heard a man scream like this before in her life. It was terrifyingly horrific and downright ugly. Trina hopped down each step one by one trying to make as little noise as possible. With all the screaming and commotion that was going on in the basement Trina was sure that the noise had drowned out any sound she had made coming down to the bottom of the steps.

Trina looked around and immediately spotted Dez laying strapped down to a table. Over him stood a shirtless Tom and in his hands he held a smoking hot iron. The smell of burnt flesh lingered throughout the air and the sound of sizzling flesh that remained stuck to the iron fried, sizzled, and popped lightly. The sight alone was enough to make a person throw up. Around Tom were several tools he planned on using as deadly weapons.

"Don't cry now motherfucker!" Tom growled and then pressed the iron down and smashed it against Dez's already skinless chest. He smiled as he held it there for at least seven seconds, and then finally removed it. "We just getting started." Tom chuckled and then turned and unplugged the iron and sat it down on the table. He took a second to look over all of the tools that lay in front of him before settling on a pair of hedge clippers.

"Now we about to really have some fun," Tom said as he eyed Dez's naked body from head to toe. His eyes then stopped when they made contact with Dez's manhood that hung between his legs. "Ohhhh," he said sarcastically. "What have we here?" he said with a sickening laugh followed behind his last comment. Just as Tom prepared to do the unthinkable a female's voice stopped him dead in his tracks.

"Guess who motherfucker!" Trina growled with a lot of hurt and emotion in her voice. Finally she had Tom right where she wanted him. "Turn your punk ass around!" she barked.

Tom turned around slowly with a smile on his face. His eyes went down to the gun that Trina held in her hand, then back up to her face. Tom spit on the floor and then spoke. "Fuck you going to do with that gun?"

"Take another step and you'll find out," Trina replied quickly. She peered past Tom and saw Dez crane his neck up and look at her through his good eye, the one that wasn't closed shut. The sight of Trina holding Tom at gun point brought a smile to Dez's bruised and battered face.

Tom sat the hedge clippers down on the table, picked up a knife, and made eye contact with Trina. This started an intense stare down that was sure to turn out deadly. "You and your father are really starting to become a pain in my ass!" Tom growled and then slowly began walking toward Trina.

"Don't take another step!" Trina warned. Tom ignored the warning and continued to slowly make his way over towards Trina with a firm grip on the handle of the knife he held in his hand.

"I said get back!" Trina yelled aiming the .22 at Tom's face.

"Make me!" Tom shot back still moving towards the teenage girl. He didn't think or feel that she had the heart to shoot him at point blank range and he didn't think that a bullet from a .22 could stop him; slow him down maybe, but not stop him. When Tom felt like he was in a close enough range to make a move he didn't hesitate. With the quickness of a cat Tom lunged towards Trina. The sound of the handgun discharging filled the basement. Tom's head violently jerked back as his body roughly and noisily collapsed face first down to the floor. Trina stood over Tom's body and fired the last two remaining bullets into the back of his head. Tears ran down Trina's cheeks. Finally, it was over! Finally Tom, his wife, and all his buddies were dead. Trina and Dez had survived. They survived the woods, the wild life dangerous animals, and most importantly they had survived the evilest, nastiest, and meanest people to ever walk the face of the earth.

Trina looked down at Tom's dead body and spit on him. "That's for my mother and brother!"

"It's over!" Dez said breaking Trina out of her trance. "It's all over baby."

Trina dropped the .22 down to the floor, walked over to the table that held all of the tools, grabbed a pair of sharp scissors, and cut the straps away from Dez's wrist and ankles. Both Dez and Trina were naked, but carried on as if they were fully dressed. Dez pulled Trina in close and hugged her tightly. "Thank you so much," he whispered in her ear.

"I did the best I could," Trina sobbed. She was in severe pain, but that's not why she was crying. She was crying because she felt that everything that had went down in the last few days was all for nothing. What was the cause for all the bloodshed?

"You did great baby," Dez assured her. "And I'm very proud of you and I know your brother and mother would be proud of you too."

"Can we please get up out of here before something else bad happens?" Trina said heading towards the stairs that led to the exit. "I can't take another surprise right now," she said seriously.

Dez followed Trina's lead, but then stopped short and headed back towards Tom's dead body.

"What are you doing? He's already dead," Trina called from the steps. "Let's get out of here."

Dez walked towards Tom's dead body, bent down, and fished through the dead man's pockets until he found what he was looking for. Dez raised his hand high in the air. A smile spread across Trina's face when she saw the tow-truck keys dangling from his hand.

"Now we can go."

Dez helped Trina up the basement steps. He was hurt and had injuries, but he was in way better condition than Trina and had to be strong enough for the both of them right now.

Once back upstairs in the middle level of the house, Dez walked to the kitchen, grabbed a sharp kitchen knife, and handed it to Trina. "Wait right here. I'll be back in a second."

"Where you going?" Trina said with a scared look on her face. After everything that had went down she never wanted to leave Dez's side again. "I'm going with you."

"I'm a run upstairs real quick and grab us some clothes for us to throw on real quick." He nodded towards her bare chest. "Don't wanna run out of here asking for help butt naked," he told her. "I'll be back in a second and stay off that ankle of yours until I get back."

Before Dez could leave, Trina grabbed his wrist and looked him in his eyes. "Please hurry back."

Dez replied with a simple head nod, and then disappeared up the stairs to go take care of the task that lay ahead of him.

Trina stood in the living room holding the kitchen knife tightly. She did her best to not look at Little Dezzy, who still sat tied down to the chair that he had been murdered in. Trina still couldn't understand how a person could do something like that to an innocent child and have no remorse. When they had arrived at the house, the place looked immaculate. Now the place looked a hot mess. One wouldn't even think it was the same house at first glance.

As Trina stood waiting for Dez to handle his business upstairs, she heard a sudden noise. A few seconds passed then she heard the noise again. Trina's eyes followed the noise and stopped at what looked to be a linen closet. She stared at the closet for a few more seconds and waited for something to jump out the closet and devour her.

"Fuck that," Trina shook her head and then hobbled as far away from the linen closet as possible. She couldn't take another surprise right now, so whatever was in that linen closet would just have to stay there. Trina was curious to see what was behind the door of the linen closet, but she wasn't curious enough to go open the door and see what was inside herself. It wasn't that much curiosity in the world. Trina looked up at the ceiling and could hear Dez upstairs moving around. *"Come on Dez. Hurry up so we can get the fuck up out of here,"* she thought.

THE GREAT ESCAPE

Upstairs Dez entered what he assumed to be Tom and Ann's bedroom. The room was well decorated with nice expensive looking furniture. Dez stepped further inside the bedroom and had to stop himself from throwing up. Pictures of victims of all nationalities hung from the walls. Pictures of their victims being tortured, being violated, being brutalized, and begging for their lives stared at Dez. Dez did his best to ignore the gruesome pictures that hung from the wall as he centered the couple's walk-in closet. The first thing Dez spotted was a pair of black slacks hanging from a plastic hanger. He snatched the too big slacks from off the hanger and slipped them on his naked waist. Then he grabbed a belt, slipped it through all the loops, and tied it tight enough around his waist to keep the slacks held up. The next thing Dez saw was a stack of wife beaters folded in a neat stack over in the corner. He grabbed one of the wife beaters, slipped it over his head, and put it on. This wasn't an outfit that Dez would normally wear or ever be caught dead in on a regular basis, but this definitely wasn't a regular basis. This was life or death, survival of the fittest, and Dez didn't want to remain in Tom's house a second longer than he had or needed to.

Dez made his way back downstairs to the living room and handed Trina a mini skirt with an elastic waistband and a sweat shirt that swallowed her whole.

"I heard something over there," Trina said once the sweat shirt was over her head.

"Huh?"

"In the linen closet," Trina said pointing towards the closet.

"You wanna go see what's in there?" Dez asked with a raised brow.

Trina quickly shook her head no.

"Didn't think so," Dez replied as he helped Trina out the front door. When Dez and Trina reached the tow-truck they both looked at each other and smiled. They were so close to the finish line they could see it, so close that they could taste it, and so close that they could feel it. Dez helped Trina up into the passenger seat of the tow-truck and then hopped in the driver seat behind the wheel. He stuck the key in the ignition, gave it a turn, and smiled when the engine rambled to life.

"We did it," Dez said smiling from ear to ear as the tow-truck pulled out of Tom's driveway and headed down the dirt road. "We did it," he repeated. Tears filled his eyes the further and further away from the house the tow-truck made it.

"What's wrong Daddy?" Trina asked when she noticed the tears streaming down her father's face. "Why are you crying?"

"I'm sorry baby," he apologized. "I just wish there was a way that I could have somehow saved Mommy and Little Dezzy. I feel as if I just left them there, left them stranded, left them abandoned, and left them there to die," he explained.

"Look at me!" Trina snapped causing Dez to take his eyes off the road and turn and face his daughter. "This is not your fault, so don't go blaming yourself. You did everything you possibly could to save us all, so don't go beating yourself up about something that was out of your control. You did your best and that's all that any of us can ask for."

"I know," was what Dez's mouth said, but his eyes and body language told a different story, a story that couldn't be edited or rewritten. It was only natural for him to beat himself up for not being able to save his wife and son. He was a man and that's what men did, they were protectors and when a man can't protect his loved ones he begins to doubt himself and his actions. He begins to ask himself had he done everything in his power to stop the situation from going bad.

"You did your best," Trina said sincerely. Her words were coming straight from the heart. She hated to see her father like this, especially after going through and seeing everything that had taken place. Trina had been with him by his side the entire way.

159

She saw the struggle, saw his effort, and saw how hard he fought to save everyone's life. She saw him risk his own life to try and save hers.

"My best wasn't good enough," Dez said in a defeated tone.

After an hour drive Dez and Trina finally spotted a small diner. A few cars sat parked in the parking lot, letting them know that the place was open for business.

"We made it!" Trina smiled and gave Dez a fist bump. Dez pulled the tow truck into the parking lot, turned off the engine, hopped down from the driver's seat, walked around the truck, and helped Trina down out of the truck.

Dez and Trina stepped foot inside the small diner and the bell at the top of the front door announced their arrival. Immediately all eyes were on the black man and the teenage girl. The patrons who sat in the restaurant all whispered and spoke in hushed voices as their eyes shot daggers through the black couple. Dez paid the weird and nasty looks no mind as he continued to help Trina over to the front counter.

"Um, may I help you?" A blonde who stood in front of an old school cash register asked with a nervous and frightened look on her face like she would be robbed at any moment.

"Yes ma'am," Dez said politely. "A cell phone, I need to use your cell phone for a second."

"Um, I don't have a cell phone," the blonde replied with a nervous and scared look still on her face. She made sure she avoided eye contact with the man that stood before her. Dez looked down at the cell phone that was clipped to the belt that resided on her waist and then back up to the white woman's face.

"You have a cell phone right there," Dez pointed out with a sign of aggravation beginning to show on his face. His lips slowly turned into a nasty scowl. "It's an emergency and it will only take a second," he told her a little more aggressively than he may have meant to.

The blonde woman quickly backpedaled toward the door that had a sign on it that said, *Employees Only.*

160

As Trina stood there waiting for the waitress to return from the back, the smell of fresh coffee and cooked food attacked her nostrils. Trina hobbled over towards an older white couples table and before they got a chance to protest her hand shot out and grabbed food straight from off one of the plates and stuffed as much food in her mouth as she could at one time. Trina moaned and made hungry sounds as she chewed her food. At that very moment this was the best food Trina had ever tasted, especially since she thought she would never taste regular cooked food ever again. The older white couple hopped up like someone had set fire to their asses and quickly rushed out of the restaurant, praying that all the black couple wanted from them was the plate of food that remained on the table and nothing else.

Dez looked at Trina, smiled, and shook his head. All he could do was laugh. His daughter was definitely a piece of work and was sure to be a handful for any man that dared to take on the responsibility of being her boyfriend in the future. Before Dez got a chance to say something to Trina about her actions, the blonde reappeared from the back with a white man that Dez assumed to be the manager.

"Hey my name is Nick and I'm the manager here," he said with a friendly I want no trouble smile on his face.

"I really need to use the phone. Me and my daughter had a really rough night and we need some medical attention and we need to speak with the police," Dez told him.

Nick peered over Dez's shoulder and saw Tom's tow truck sitting out front. "You know Tom?" Nick asked with a suspicious look on his face nodding towards the tow truck outside.

"I need to speak to the police," Dez repeated as calm as possible. His patience was running thin and the urge to break Nick's jaw was getting stronger and stronger with each passing second.

"You not here to start no trouble right? Tommy is good people and I know he would never let you people use his truck. Where's Tom? Is he okay? What did y'all do to him?" Nick said firing question after question at the black man that stood on the other side of the counter. "What did you do to Tom?"

"Motherfucker!" Dez barked. "I just told you I need to use the phone to call the police. Now either you call the police or I'm going to hop across the counter, whip yo ass, grab that phone, and call myself."

Nick stood there for a second with a dumb look on his face, looking as if he was weighing his options, and then suddenly he spoke. "Listen why don't you and your friend go have a seat and I'll have Amanda here," he nodded towards the blonde. "Bring you over some food and I'll get on the phone and call the sheriff. How does that sound?"

"Thank you Nick," Dez said then grabbed Trina and headed over to a vacant table. After everything Dez have been through he was starting to hate white people. Their first impression of a black man was always a negative one and he hated that. Of course there were a lot of ignorant black people out in the world, but that didn't mean that they were all ignorant and the ones that were ignorant chose to be that way.

"What did he say?" Trina asked.

"Said he's going to call the sheriff for us." Dez smiled as he looked pass the counter and saw Nick on the phone. He just hoped and prayed that he was in fact calling the sheriff and not someone else. "We'll sit and enjoy a nice hot meal until the sheriff arrives."

Trina got ready to reply to what Dez had said when she looked around and saw that all eyes were on her. "I mean damn!" she huffed. "What the fuck is everyone looking at? What y'all never seen black people before? Damn!"

"Calm down baby," Dez said in a calm tone as Amanda walked up to their table with a phony smile on her face.

"Are y'all ready to order?" She held a small pencil and small pad in her hand and scribbled down both Dez and Trina's order and then spun off.

"And don't spit in our shit either!" Trina said to Amanda's departing back.

162

As Dez waited for Amanda to return with their food he unconsciously kept glancing back and forth out the window hoping to see the sheriff's car pull into the parking lot.

"You think they really called the sheriff?" Trina asked skeptically.

"We'll find out soon enough," was Dez's response.

THE SHERIFF

ez stared up at the clock that rested in the center of the wall and noticed that two hours had passed and there was still no sign of the sheriff. He discreetly snatched the steak knife from off his plate and slipped it down in his pocket. He was getting ready to do some serious bodily harm to Nick and maybe even Amanda if need be. Dez stood up with his hand tightly gripped around the handle of the steak knife down in his pocket and started over towards the counter, but stopped in his tracks when he heard Trina say, "Look."

Dez stopped and turned towards the window and felt a sigh of relief when he saw the sheriff's car pull into the parking lot. "About time," he murmured.

Dez and Trina met the sheriff outside not even bothering to wait for him to enter the diner. Nick followed close behind the couple. He was so glad that the sheriff had finally arrived. Nick was beginning to feel as if the black man was going to do something to him if the sheriff hadn't arrived when he did.

"Sheriff Smith," the sheriff introduced himself to the black man and black teenage girl that stood before him. The first thing Sheriff Smith did was take in Dez and Trina's appearance. After just a glance, the sheriff could tell that the two had been through a lot, maybe more than he could even imagine. "What seems to be the problem?"

Before Dez could even reply to the sheriff, Nick barged in. "He's done something to Tom and his wife," Nick blurted out. "He pulled up in Tom's truck and I know for a fact that Tom would never let someone like him borrow his work truck."

Sheriff Smith turned and faced Dez. "Mind telling me how you got a hold of Tom's tow truck?" He now eyed Dez suspiciously.

"Tom and his wife along with a few of his buddies killed my wife and son," Dez told the Sheriff. "Me and my daughter here have been stranded and held captive for the past two or three days out in the middle of nowhere."

"So you're telling me that Tom and his lovely wife killed your family?" the sheriff asked.

"Yes!"

"But you still never answered how you got his work truck," the sheriff pointed out with his hand inching closer and closer towards the service pistol that was glued to his hip down in its holster.

"Look!" Trina jumped into the conversation. "We killed Tom! We killed Ann and we killed everyone associated with them!" she told the sheriff. "Tom killed my mother and my brother and he even tried to kill me." She nodded down towards her ankle. "We did what we had to do plain and simple!"

At that moment Dez wished Trina would shut up and let him do all the talking because she was digging them into an even deeper hole.

"Sheriff Smith," Dez intervened. "Me and my daughter need medical attention. I'm sure once you do your investigation, you'll find out that our story is authentic," he assured him.

"Let me start off by saying that I know Tom and Ann personally and they're not the monsters that y'all are depicting them to be," Sheriff Smith said in a matter of fact tone. "I don't know what kind of game the two of you are playing, but if I don't get the truth in the next ten seconds, I'm going to haul both of y'all asses off to jail!"

"Get the truth?" Trina echoed looking at the Sheriff like he was insane. "We just told you that Tom and his wife held us captive and tortured us for the last few days and you're about to take us to jail? Nah, fuck that!"

"Listen here!" Sheriff Smith yelled with his index finger pointed at Trina. "You just told me that the two of you just killed Tom and his wife and I'm just trying to get to the bottom of the situation," he explained.

"Get down to the bottom of the situation?" Trina repeated. Dez tried to calm her down, but she was already two turned up to be turned down right now. "Look at my ankle!" Trina barked. "Let me guess, I did this to my own ankle right? I did this to myself to right?" She lifted up her shirt revealing all the fresh nasty scars, whelps, and bruises that covered her body.

"Listen Sheriff," Dez stepped in before Trina got them both put in jail out in the middle of nowhere. "We can all take a ride back down to Tom's house and that way you can verify our story. Tom burned my son to a crisp and chopped my wife's head off then sat it on the kitchen counter like it was a souvenir." he explained with the cooler head. "My wife and son's body is still at Tom's house. Once you verify this then can we move on and get us some medical attention and get us back to our home?"

"Once your story is verified, I promise I'll get you and your daughter some medical attention and you'll be free to go," Sheriff Smith said opening up the back door for Dez and Trina.

"I don't trust this cracker," Trina whispered not budging.

"Neither do I, but right now this is our only option." Dez grabbed Trina's hand and led her to the sheriff's car and then helped her inside. "We gon be alright," he whispered in her ear.

"You promise?"

"I promise."

Sheriff Smith hopped in the front seat of the cruiser and just like that Dez and Trina were headed right back to the same house that they had fought so hard to get away from.

Sheriff Smith and Dez's eyes met briefly in the rearview mirror for a split second and then he spoke. "It's not that I don't believe you two's story, it's just something I have to look into myself," he smirked. "This isn't something that I could just take at face value you know?"

"Whatever," Trina mumbled. She was immediately turned off and disgusted by the Sheriff and how he was taking care of the situation at hand and she wasn't afraid to let him know about himself.

"Just doing my job," Sheriff Smith said and then the conversation was left at that. The rest of the ride was a silent one. Dez and Trina both were just ready for this nightmare to finally be over and done with.

HOME SWEET HOME

S heriff Smith pulled the cruiser up in front of Tom's house and killed the engine. "Okay here we are," he announced opening the back door so Dez and Trina could get out.

"My daughter is badly injured. Is it really necessary for us to get out?" Dez asked. "I'm sure you don't need us for your investigation."

"Actually I do," Sheriff Smith replied. "I want y'all to show me these dead bodies that y'all were telling me about. It'll only take a second."

Dez and Trina reluctantly got out the back seat of the cruiser and followed Sheriff Smith to the front of the house. The Sheriff grabbed the door knob, gave it a light turn, and then entered the house. "Okay now show me where all these bodies y'all were telling me about are located."

Dez and Trina both entered the house and couldn't believe their eyes. The living room that once looked like a tornado had run through it twice was now spotless. The place was so clean that it looked like a person could eat off the floor.

"Nah, there's got to be some kind of mistake," Dez said not understanding what was going on. He and Trina had left this same house no longer than three hours ago and didn't understand how or who for that matter had cleaned up the house and removed the bodies. "Somebody is trying to set us up," Dez exclaimed. There was no other explanation for what was going on. Dead bodies didn't move on their own, nor did they get up and walk away. Someone cleaned up the house and removed the dead bodies from the premises.

"Okay you two got some explaining to do," Sheriff Smith said looking at both Trina and Dez for answers. "Get to talking."

"Somebody is trying to set us up," Dez told him. "I swear my son's body was right there tied down to a chair."

"You want to know what I think?" Sheriff Smith said. "I think the two of you done fucked with the wrong one this time," he said then quickly pulled his .357 from his holster and aimed it at Dez.

"Hold on a minute Sheriff," Dez said throwing his hands up in surrender. "I swear to God we're innocent. Tom killed my son."

"And you killed mines," the Sheriff capped back.

Dez looked confused. He had never seen the Sheriff a day in his life so he must have had him mistaken with someone else. "I think you got me confused with someone else."

A stone cold expression sat on the Sheriff's face. "I told Tom about playing this stupid ass game with his victims. Yes he was hard headed, but you didn't have to kill him."

"Your Tom's father?" Dez asked not believing his ears.

"How else you think he got away with this for so many years?" The Sheriff nodded down at the gold badge that rested on his chest. "We had a nice little system going on and then you came along and fucked that up."

"You people are sick," Dez said with a disgusted look on his face. "Tom is a bitch just like his father."

"Down in the basement," Sheriff Smith ordered. "I'm going to finish just what my son started."

Dez and Trina both stood frozen in place. There was no way either one of them were going back into that basement. Sheriff Smith would have to shoot them both dead right where they stood and then drag them down in the basement. That was the only way he was going to get the father and daughter duo down there again. Dez thought about reaching for the steak knife that rested in his pocket, but knew by the time he got the knife out of his pocket, the sheriff would've already filled him with holes.

"I said down in the basement. Now!" Sheriff Smith barked.

Dez was about to tell the Sheriff to go fuck himself until he spotted a figure over Sheriff Smith's shoulder exit the linen closet approaching with a shiny object in his or her hands.

"You can take that gun and shove it up your white ass!" Dez said as Trina burst out laughing. Before the Sheriff got a chance to respond the figure behind him brought an ax down with great force. The ax cut through the air and landed in the back of Sheriff Smith's head making a loud squishing thudding sound. Dez and Trina both watched as the Sheriff fell face first down to the floor. Behind the Sheriff stood Frankie. Immediately Dez walked up to Frankie and hugged her tightly as if he was trying to squeeze the air out of her. "Thank you so much," he whispered in her ear.

Trina cleared her throat getting Dez and Frankie's attention. "Want to introduce me to your friend?" she asked with a smile.

"Frankie this is my daughter Trina and Trina this is my friend Frankie," Dez said introducing the two.

Trina hobbled over towards Frankie and gave her a big hug. "Thank you for helping us out. I really appreciate it."

"Don't mention it," Frankie replied coolly. She was just happy to see Dez reunited with his daughter. "Your father really loves you," she told Trina.

"I know he does," Trina smiled. "And I love him too."

Dez searched through Sheriff Smith's pockets until he found the keys to the cruiser. It was finally all over. Dez, Trina, and Frankie has survived. They were the last one's standing and they made it to the end. "We did it," Dez announced. "It's finally over!"

"No, it ain't over yet," Frankie said. Then she grabbed the back of Dez's head with two hands and kissed Dez like he belonged to her; a long sloppy drawn out kiss. "I'll say we're just getting started." Frankie smiled like a little schoolgirl and like that the trio headed out the front door, hopped into the cruiser, pulled off of Tom's property, and headed back to the city. Dez, Trina, and Frankie didn't ever want to see another tree or woods ever again.

"Home Sweet Home," Trina said as the trio enjoyed a nice laugh as the cruiser coasted along the Highway.

EPILOGUE
TWO YEARS LATER

D ez and Frankie both set in attendance and watched as Trina walked across the stage and received her high school diploma. Trina now walked with a slight limp, her ankle had never quite healed properly, but Trina would rather walk with a limp than not walk at all any day.

"I can't believe she did it," Dez said with watery eyes. He had to blink to keep the tears from trickling down his cheeks. At times two years ago when they were out stranded in the woods he never thought he'd ever be able to see this day with his own eyes, but here he was and right next to him sat Frankie. She wore a nice silver Vera Wang classy spaghetti strap dress, with a pair of open toe silver four inch heels. For the past two years the three had been living together and believe it or not the two year tragedy had brought all three of them so much closer to one another and Dez was just thankful to be alive. After all the media coverage their story had gotten Dez was happy that all the hype was finally starting to die down. All he wanted was to live a regular normal life. He could only imagine what the men he had left behind in prison thought when they saw him and his deranged story all over the news.

***

After the graduation ceremony, Dez took Trina and Frankie out to a five-star restaurant to celebrate such an accomplishment. Trina and Frankie laughed, joked, and gossiped like they were best friends. Dez sipped on his glass of wine while in deep thought.

Frankie leaned over and kissed Dez on the cheek. "What you over here thinking about?"

"Nothing," he answered quickly.

"We don't keep secrets from each other so spit it out." Frankie wrapped two arms around Dez's neck and kissed him repeatedly until he finally shooed her away.

"Alright, alright, alright," Dez said. He looked back and forth from Frankie to Trina. "I was thinking about having our story told."

Trina and Frankie both smiled. "Told like in a movie?" Trina asked excitedly.

"I was thinking in the form of a book first. I think our story is an interesting and unique one and I know it will keep readers entertained," Dez told them.

"Who would you get to write it?" Frankie asked.

"Well when I was locked up, I read some very good books by this author named Silk White and if anyone writes our story I want it to be him."

"Okay, I say go for it," Frankie said simply.

"I got Silk White's email address from off of Facebook and plus it's in the back of all of his books," Dez paused. "But I'm not sure if this is the type of story he'd be interested in writing."

"What kind of books does he write?" Frankie asked curiously. She herself had never heard of this author Silk White.

"Street lit," Dez answered.

Trina pulled her iPad mini from her purse and slid it over towards Dez. "There's only one way to find out. Email him and see what he says," she suggested.

Dez took the iPad and stared at it for a second like he was making a life or death decision.

"Fuck it," Dez said. "It doesn't hurt to try. The only thing he could say is no." He typed Silk White a brief email and then looked up at Trina and Frankie. "Keep your fingers crossed." Dez smiled and then pressed the send button.

Now Available:
Paperback & E-Book

On Our Bookshelf

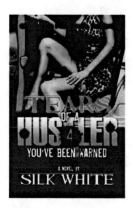

Good2Go Films Presents

174

To order films please go to www.good2gofilms.com
To order books, please fill out the order form below:

Name: _____

Address:

_____

City: _____ State: _____ Zip Code: _____

Phone:_____

Email: _____

Method Payment:

Check ☐   VISA ☐   MASTERCARD ☐

Credit Card#: _____

Name as it appears on card: _____

Signature: _____

Item Name	Price	Qty	Amount
Slumped – Jason Brent	$14.95		
He Loves Me, He Loves You Not - Mychea	$14.95		
He Loves Me, He Loves You Not 2 - Mychea	$14.95		
Married To Da Streets – Silk White	$14.95		
Never Be The Same – Silk White	$14.95		
Tears of a Hustler - Silk White	$14.95		
Tears of a Hustler 2 - Silk White	$14.95		
Tears of a Hustler 3 - Silk White	$14.95		
Tears of a Hustler 4- Silk White	$14.95		
The Teflon Queen – Silk White	$14.95		
The Teflon Queen 2 – Silk White	$14.95		
Young Goonz – Reality Way	$14.95		
Tears of a Hustler 5 – Silk White	$14.95		
Subtotal:			
Tax:			
Shipping (Free) U.S. Media Mail:			
Total:			

Make Checks Payable To:
Good2Go Publishing
7311 W Glass Lane
Laveen, AZ 85339

CPSIA information can be obtained at www.ICGtesting.com
Printed in the USA
LVOW07s2009070116

469670LV00018B/808/P